GEORGE ORWELL'S ANIMAL FARM

PETER HALL was born in 1930 and educated at St. Catharine's College, Cambridge, where he directed more than twenty stage productions. Subsequently, his professional stage work includes directing eighteen of Shakespeare's plays at Stratford-upon-Avon; the premieres of plays by Samuel Beckett, Edward Albee, Jean Anouilh, Peter Shaffer, John Mortimer and John Whiting; and the first productions of seven Harold Pinter plays. He has also directed operas at Covent Garden, Glyndebourne, the Metropolitan Opera, New York, Geneva and Bayreuth, as well as seven films, including *Akenfield*. He founded The Royal Shakespeare Company in 1960 and ran it until 1968. He has been the Director of the National Theatre since 1973, and the Artistic Director of Glyndebourne since 1984.

GEORGE ORWELL was born in India in 1903. Educated in England, he then served in the Indian Imperial Police in Burma from 1922 to 1928. Following this, his first book, *Down and Out in Paris and London* (1933) was written out of his experiences of near destitution in those cities. In *The Road to Wigan Pier* (1937) he investigated the conditions of the unemployed in the North of England; and *Homage to Catalonia* (1938) was an account of the Spanish Civil War written again from personal experience and deep commitment. He had written three novels by 1936 including *Burmese Days* (1933) and *Keep the Aspidistra Flying* (1936), but *Coming Up for Air* (1939) is considered his best pre-war novel. After the outbreak of World War Two he wrote articles for several newspapers and journals — particularly a weekly column in *The Tribune* — and his book *The Lion and the Unicorn* (1941), all of which reflected his belief in the need for social revolution in Britain. In 1945 he received widespread public acclaim for his political allegory, *Animal Farm*. Just before his death in 1950 came publication of his most famous novel, *1984*.

George Orwell's

ANIMAL FARM

adapted by Peter Hall

with lyrics by Adrian Mitchell
and music by Richard Peaslee

Methuen · London

A METHUEN PAPERBACK

First published as a Methuen Paperback original in 1985
by Methuen London Ltd, 11 New Fetter Lane, London EC4P 4EE
Reprinted 1988

Dramatic adaptation copyright © Peter Hall 1985
Lyrics copyright © Adrian Mitchell 1985
Music copyright © Richard Peaslee 1985

Set in IBM 9pt Press Roman by 🅵\Tek-Art, Croydon, Surrey
Printed in Great Britain

ISBN 0 413 60060 2

CAUTION

Animal Farm was first performed at the Cottesloe Theatre, London, on 25 April 1984 by the National Theatre with the following cast:

BOXER/FARMER	Geoffrey Burridge
CAT/NAPOLEON'S DOG/HEN/PIGEONS	Kate Dyson
HEN/COW/MRS JONES/PIG	Jenny Galloway
THE BOY	Kamlesh Gupta/
	Christopher Howard
SNOWBALL/MR WHYMPER	Greg Hicks
MR JONES/GOOSE	Paul Imbusch
OLD MAJOR/MR PILKINGTON/SHEEP	Kenny Ireland
SHEEP/FARMER	Bill Moody
MINIMUS/HEN	Wendy Morgan
MURIEL	Judith Paris
NAPOLEON	Barrie Rutter
SQUEALER	David Ryall
CLOVER	Dinah Stabb
MOSES/HEN/PIGEONS/FARMER	Paul Stewart
COW/PIG/STABLE LAD	Paul Tomany
MOLLIE/NAPOLEON'S DOG/HEN	Jessica Turner
BENJAMIN	Bev Willis

Directed by Peter Hall
Decor and masks by Jennifer Carey
Lighting by John Bury
Movement by Stuart Hopps
Musical direction by Matthew Scott
Sound by Caz Appleton

Animal Farm was subsequently performed in repertoire at the Olivier Theatre from 27 September 1984 to 3 April 1985 with a slightly altered cast. It returned to the repertoire in the Lyttleton Theatre on 2 September 1985 prior to a nine-city tour in autumn 1985 to Cardiff, Nottingham, Norwich, Bath, Plymouth, Manchester, Wolverhampton, Belfast and Hull.

A Note by the Adaptor

With judicious doubling, the play can be presented by a dozen actors. If more actors are available, they can be used to fill out the chorus of animals.

The original stage was completely black. Brightly coloured elements of the Farm — like pieces in a child's toy set — were moved about by black figures. The actors wore black, except for brightly coloured elements — their animal masks, tails and feet. Until the end of the play, they went on all fours, using crutches of varying heights on their hands. The 'human' characters also wore masks. This was one solution to the production of the play. There are many others.

Peter Hall
January 1985

ACT ONE

A BOY's *bedroom. A large bookcase. A toy chest on it, a child's brightly coloured farm set.*

A BOY *some eight or nine years old strolls forward. He stands on a chair and selects a book from the top of the bookcase. He moves down stage and sits on the toy box.*

BOY (*reading*): *Animal Farm.* A fairy story by George Orwell.
The BOY's *room disappears. The farmhouse, and the farm gate take over the stage.* MR JONES *is revealed standing by the gate. On the gate is painted a slogan: 'Manor Farm'.* 'In the past Mr Jones, although a cruel master, had been a capable farmer. But now he spent more and more time in the Red Lion. Every night he came home drunk.

MR JONES (*singing*): **Who made the cows and sheep so meek?**
Who feeds the cats and dogs their meat?
Who's the loving father
Of fur and feather?
Man, bounteous man! Wonderful man!

BOY: His farm was now thoroughly neglected. The fields were full of weeds and the animals were underfed and in poor condition.

MR JONES: **Who guards his servants with a gun**
And, when their time to leave has come,
Who leads pigs and horses
To slaughter houses?
Man, masterful man. Powerful man.

BOY: He went up the stairs, undressed and climbed unsteadily into bed.
Throughout the play what the BOY *describes happens around him. The black figures set elements of the farm, become animals, execute mimes, or speak scenes of dialogue.*
JONES *makes his way to the door of his house, kicks off his boots, and, still singing, goes up the stairs. Finally, the bedroom light goes out.*

BOY: As soon as the light was out, there was a stirring and a fluttering throughout the farm. Word had gone round the animals that there was to be a secret meeting in the big barn. Old Major, the stud boar had something to say. . . .

Lights up on the barn full of animals. OLD MAJOR, *a large old pig, centre stage.* HENS, PIGEONS, SHEEP, COWS; BOXER, *a huge cart horse;* CLOVER, *a stout motherly mare;* MURIEL, *the white goat;* BENJAMIN, *the old donkey.*

MAJOR: Last night I had a strange dream. Many years ago when I was a little pig, my mother and the other sows used to sing a secret and ancient song. I learnt that song. I learnt its words, I learnt its music. But it has long since passed out of my mind. Last night it came back to me. In my dream. . . .

(He sings:) **Beasts of England! Beasts of Ireland!**
Beasts of land and sea and skies!
Hear the hoofbeats of tomorrow!
See the golden future rise!
The animals stir, but he quietens them.

Wait — no noise — wait! Or we'll wake up Jones! I am over twelve years old and have had over four hundred children. I think I understand the nature of life on this earth as well as any animal now living. Listen carefully, for I do not think that I shall be with you for many months longer.
MOLLIE, *a foolish pretty white mare, rushes in late.*

CLOVER: Why are you late, Mollie?

MOLLIE: Sorry . . . I had a stone in my hoof. *(She shrugs girlishly.)*

MAJOR: Listen!

(He sings:) **How does the life of an animal pass?**
In endless drudgery.
What's the first lesson an animal learns?
To endure its slavery.
How does the life of an animal end?
In cruel butchery.

Is this simply part of the order of nature? No, Comrades. This farm would support a dozen horses, twenty cows, hundreds of sheep — all of them living in comfort and dignity beyond our imagining. Our labour tills the soil, our dung fertilises it. And yet there is not one of us who owns more than his bare skin. The produce of our labour is stolen from us by human beings. Man is our only enemy.
He's the lord of all the animals
Yet he can't lay eggs or pull a plough.

He's the greatest of all criminals,
Stealing wool from the sheep and milk from the cow.
He's the lord of all the animals
And the only one who's no use.
For he consumes, consumes, consumes,
But he cannot produce.

Never listen when they tell you that man and the animals have a common interest — that the prosperity of the one is the prosperity of the other. You cows: what has happened to the milk which should feed you calves?

THE COWS: It has gone down the throat of our enemy! Man!

MAJOR: And you hens: what has happened to the eggs you have laid?

THE HENS: They have been stolen from us by our enemy! Man!

MAJOR: And you, Clover: where are your six children, the foals who should have been the support and pleasure of your old age?

CLOVER: They were sold at a year old by our enemy, man! I will never see them again.

MAJOR: But even the miserable lives that we lead are not allowed to reach their natural span. You young pigs will scream your lives out on the block within a year — every one of you.

YOUNG PIGS (*in terror*): No! No! No!

MAJOR: Yes! To that horror we must all come. Cows, pigs, hens, sheep, everyone — even you Boxer. They'll butcher you.

BOXER: Why me? I work hard for them.

MAJOR: The day that those great muscles of yours lose their power, Jones will sell you to the knacker, who will cut your throat and boil you down for dog food. What must we do? Why, work, comrades. Work night and day, body and soul, for the overthrow of the human race! Rebellion! That is my message to you, comrades! Rebellion! I do not know when the rebellion will come, but I know as surely as I see the straw beneath my feet that sooner or later justice will be done. But when you conquer man do not adopt his vices. Remember that all animals are equal!

SNOWBALL: Old Major, what about the wild creatures — the rats and the rabbits — are they our friends or our enemies?

MAJOR: You must decide. You must learn to vote. Each one of

you must have a say in the way lead our lives. I propose
this question to the meeting: Are the wild creatures
comrades? All those in favour . . .
*They begin to take a vote by raising their trotters and
hooves. As the* BOY *speaks the action freezes.*

BOY: And so the animals learnt to vote for the first time. It was
agreed by an overwhelming majority that the wild creatures
were comrades.

ALL THE ANIMALS: Agreed, agreed!

BOY: There was only one vote against: the cat. She was
afterwards discovered to have voted on both sides.

MAJOR *and all the* ANIMALS: **Beasts of England! Beasts of
Ireland!**
Beasts of land and sea and skies!
Hear the hoofbeats of tomorrow!
See the golden future rise!

Now the day of beasts is coming,
Tyrant man shall lose his throne
And the shining fields of England
Shall be trod by beasts alone.

Pull the rings from out of your noses!
Tear the saddle from your back!
Bit and spur shall rust forever,
Cruel whips no more shall crack.

Beasts of England, seize the prizes,
Wheat and barley, oats and hay,
Clover, beans and mangel wurzels
Shall be ours upon that day,
Shall be ours upon that —

MR JONES *flings open his bedroom window*

MR JONES (*shouting*): QU-I-ET!
The ANIMALS *freeze, holding their breath.*

What's bothering you? Is it a fox? A fox, is it?
He reaches for his shotgun and fires into the darkness.
The lights fade as the meeting of the ANIMALS *breaks
up quickly and silently.*

BOY: Three nights later, Old Major died peacefully in his sleep.
The ANIMALS *watch as* OLD MAJOR *slowly leaves.*
His body was buried at the foot of the orchard.

Lights up. MR JONES *moves among the* ANIMALS, *cracking his whip.*

During the next three months, Jones continued to starve and bully them. But now the animals had a secret. They did not know when to expect the rebellion, but they believed fervently that one day it would come. The pigs, being the cleverest of the animals, led the preparation by organising and teaching.

NAPOLEON, SNOWBALL *and* SQUEALER *are seen teaching the* ANIMALS.

These three — Snowball, Squealer and Napoleon — had elaborated Old Major's teachings into a complete system of thought to which they gave the name. . . .

NAPOLEON, SNOWBALL *and* SQUEALER (*singing*):
Animalism . . ! Animalism . . ! Animalism . . !

ALL THE ANIMALS: **Animalism!**

BOY: Snowball was an idealist, a pig who always dreamt of perfecting the future . . .

SNOWBALL: A spectre is haunting England: the spectre of Animalism. Animalism will lead us to the life of plenty. Everything that we produce, we shall own — collectively.

BOY: Squealer loved to talk . . .

SQUEALER: Information, comrades; facts, comrades; these are the foundations of Animalism. Without knowledge, we can have no opinions. And unless we have opinions, we cannot vote. The majority must rule.

BOY: And Napoleon was a pig they all trusted . . .

NAPOLEON: I'm a practical pig, a pig of few words. So I'll work hard and say little.

BOY: After Mr Jones was asleep, they all held secret meetings in the barn.
SNOWBALL, SQUEALER *and* NAPOLEON *are holding their meeting. They sing.*

SNOWBALL: **No man**
No master

SQUEALER: **Animals help each other.**

NAPOLEON: **Work fast**
Work faster

SNOWBALL: **Work for the future, brother**

FIRST COW: But Mr Jones feeds us.

SECOND COW: If he were gone we should starve to death.

THIRD COW: So we have to be loyal.

SNOWBALL: **No! Animalism alters history!**
Two-legged creatures are the enemy!
Cows, sheep, chickens, cockerel, goose —
Animals shall eat what animals produce!

NAPOLEON: **No man**
No killing
What is our battle's sequel?

SNOWBALL (*sings*): **A land worth tilling.**
All animals are equal.

CAT: I don't care what happens after I am dead.

SHEEP: If this rebellion is going to happen anyway, why should
we work for it?

SQUEALER: Try to understand, comrades. Allow yourselves to
live by the spirit of Animalism.

SNOWBALL, SQUEALER *and* NAPOLEON: **No man**
No master
All animals are equal.

ALL THE ANIMALS: **No man**
No master
All animals are equal

MOLLIE: Will there still be sugar after the rebellion?

SNOWBALL: You don't need sugar. You will have all the oats
and hay you want.

MOLLIE: But shall I still be able to wear ribbons in my mane?

SQUEALER: Comrade, those ribbons are the badge of slavery.

SQUEALER: Don't you understand that liberty is worth more
than ribbons?

MOLLIE (*unconvinced*): Yes, I suppose so. Couldn't I have some
liberty ribbons?

BOY: The pigs had an even harder struggle to counteract the
religious stories put about by Moses, Mr Jones' tame raven.
MOSES *appears on a rafter. The* ANIMALS *quickly form*
into a respectful congregation.

MOSES (*liturgically*): Believe me brethren. It's there, up in the
sky!

Beyond the fences of this life
There lies a wondrous hill
And all good creatures when they die
Go there to graze their fill.

ALL THE ANIMALS: On Sugarcandy Mountain
No labouring is done.
Beside a milky fountain
The beasts lie in the sun.
On Sugarcandy Mountain
You'll find the Treacle Lake
Lump sugar beyond counting
And fields of linseed cake.

So fear no more the knacker's yard
Nor dread the abattoir,
But work today so you may join
That Sugarcandy Choir.

On Sugarcandy Mountain
You'll find the Treacle Lake.

SNOWBALL, SQUEALER *and* NAPOLEON (*as they break up
the meeting*): There's no such place as Sugarcandy Mountain,
No sweet by-and-by.
There's no such place as Sugarcandy Mountain,
Sugarcandy Mountain is a lie, lie, lie!
Sugarcandy Mountain is a lie!

SQUEALER: There's no such place as Sugarcandy Mountain,
Animals are slaughtered and then
Converted into pork or mutton pies
Which are guzzled down the throats of men.

ALL THE ANIMALS: There's no such place as Sugarcandy
Mountain,
When you die you die.
There's no such place as Sugarcandy Mountain,
Sugarcandy Mountain is a lie. Lie, lie, lie!
Sugarcandy Mountain is a lie!
Is a mountainous, mountainous, mountainous lie!

MOSES *leaves screaming in protest. The lights fade on the*
ANIMALS.

BOY: And so they went on waiting, waiting for the rebellion.
Finally, it came sooner than anyone expected. One Saturday,
Mr Jones got so drunk at the Red Lion that he did not come

home till Sunday. And then he forgot to feed the
animals. . . .
*MR JONES returns drunk from the village. He ignores the
pleas of the* ANIMALS, *and goes into the farmhouse.*

ALL THE ANIMALS: Food! Where's our food? Give us food!

BOY: Mr Jones immediately went to sleep on the drawing room
sofa, with the *News of the World* over his face. When
evening came, the animals were still unfed, and the
barndoors were padlocked.

ALL THE ANIMALS (*in greater anguish*): Food! Where's our
food? Give us food!

BOY: At last they could stand it no longer.
Music. BOXER *kicks the barn door open, and the*
ANIMALS *rush into it and begin to feed.* MR JONES *wakes
up and comes into the yard. He confronts the* ANIMALS
with the whip. There is a moment of stillness.
Suddenly, the ANIMALS *fling themselves upon* MR JONES
*Their sudden uprising frightens him and he takes to his
heels. He pushes open the farm gate and runs away down
the road. The* ANIMALS *slam the gate behind him.*
And so, almost before they knew it had started, the
rebellion was over. Manor Farm was theirs. They quickly
wiped out all traces of the hated Jones.
MURIEL *tears the union jack from the flag pole and eats it.*

ALL THE ANIMALS: Hooray!
BOXER *shakes off his straw hat and drops it over the gate.*
well.

BOXER: Just a gesture . . .
SNOWBALL *breaks the whip in two which* JONES *has
discarded in the fight.*

ALL THE ANIMALS: Hooray! Hooray! Hooray!
The ANIMALS *survey the farm.*

BOY: They made a tour of inspection of the whole farm and
surveyed with speechless admiration the ploughland, the
hayfield, the orchard, the pool, the spinney. It was as
though they had never seen these things before. And even
now they could hardly believe that it was all their own.
Then they filed back to the farm house and halted outside
the door.
SNOWBALL *and* NAPOLEON *kick the door open and the*
ANIMALS *cautiously enter the house.*

BOY: They tiptoed from room to room afraid to speak above a whisper. They touched with awe the unbelievable luxury — the beds, the looking glasses, the sofa, the carpets, the lithograph of Queen Victoria. Mollie found a ribbon . . .
MOLLIE takes a piece of blue ribbon from the dressing table, holds it against herself, and admires herself in the mirror.

SQUEALER: Ribbons are the mark of human beings. All animals should go naked . . .

BOY: The pigs lifted down some hams hanging in the kitchen . . .
TWO YOUNG PIGS solemnly carry the hams out of the house in their teeth.

NAPOLEON: Let us give them decent burial.
The ANIMALS *hang their heads.*

SQUEALER: I propose that this odious farmhouse should be preserved as a museum. The museum of man, the murderer. Let us put it to the vote.

ALL THE ANIMALS (*raising their trotters and hooves*): Agreed! Agreed!

SNOWBALL: I have another proposal: is it agreed that no animals shall ever live here?

ALL THE ANIMALS: Agreed! Agreed!
The lights fade. NAPOLEON *detaches himself from the rest of the animals.*

BOY: Mr Jones had four puppies, children of the guard dogs who had fled with him. Napoleon took the puppies away to a secret place, an old incubator shed behind the farmhouse. There, he fed them and looked after them. The rest of the farm soon forgot their existence.
Lights up. The ANIMALS *are all gathered round the five barred gate at the entrance to the farm.* SNOWBALL *holds a brush in his trotter. He has just finished painting a new name on the gate: 'Animal Farm'.*

BOY: And now Snowball revealed something wonderful . . .

SNOWBALL: Animal Farm!

BOXER: But how can you read? How can you write?

SQUEALER: During the time of preparation, we pigs taught ourselves to read and write . . .

SNOWBALL: From an old spelling book which belonged to Mr Jones' children . . .

NAPOLEON: We found it on the rubbish heap.

MOLLIE (*reflectively*): It's a beautiful name, Animal Farm . . .

ALL THE ANIMALS (*singing*): '**Animal Farm**'
    Lights out.

BOY: The pigs next explained that they had succeeded in
    reducing the principles of Animalism to seven
    commandments.
    Lights up on the barn. SNOWBALL *is just painting slogan
    number seven on the lowest point of the wall.*

SNOWBALL (*as he finishes painting*):	ALL THE ANIMALS (*repeating*):
One.	One.
Two-legged beings are our enemies.	Our enemies.
Two.	Two.
Four-legged beings are allies and friends.	Allies and friends.
Three.	Three.
Animals shall never wear any clothes.	Never wear clothes.
Four.	Four.
Animals shall never sleep in beds.	Never sleep in beds.
Five.	Five.
Animals shall never drink alcohol.	No alcohol.
Six.	Six.
Animals shall never kill animals.	Never kill animals.
Seven.	Seven.
All animals are equal.	All animals are equal.

SNOWBALL: These are the Seven Commandments. These
    are the unalterable Laws of Animal Farm.

ANIMALS: Hooray!

SNOWBALL: Comrades! Now that we are all equal, we are all
    equally responsible for the running of Animal Farm. So we
    must vote. And to vote, we must have opinions, be
    informed . . .

A SHEEP: So do we have a leader?

SNOWBALL: You are all leaders now. All leading Animal Farm to a bright and happy future.

ANOTHER SHEEP: But who takes the decisions?

SNOWBALL: You do.

CAT: But what if I don't agree with the other leaders?

SNOWBALL: But you will. The Majority is always right.

SHEEP: Oh good!

NAPOLEON: Don't worry, comrade. Just be practical. If we ·work hard, we shall not be hungry. And if we're not hungry, we shall worry less and argue less.

BOXER: That's right, Napoleon. Comrade Napoleon is always right.

ANIMALS: He is!

NAPOLEON: Thank you, comrades.

SNOWBALL: Now, comrades to the hayfield! Let's see if we can get the harvest in more quickly than Jones and his men. *There is a loud howl of protest from three* COWS.

FIRST COW: Wait! We haven't been milked for twenty-four hours.

SECOND COW: My udder is about to burst.

THIRD COW: We can do nothing without men.

BOY: So the pigs got buckets and milked the cows.
The PIGS *are seen milking the* COWS.
They were very successful, because their trotters were well adapted to this task.
The PIGS *are seen carrying full buckets of milk.*

ANIMALS: hooray!

MOLLIE: What will happen to all that milk?

NAPOLEON: Never mind the milk, comrades. That will be attended to. The harvest is more important. Comrade Snowball will lead the way. I shall follow in a few minutes. Forward, comrades! The hay is waiting.
The ANIMALS *troop hesitantly off to the hayfield, as the lights fade. Only the* BOY *is left illuminated.*

BOY: When they came back in the evening, the milk had disappeared. Every day it disappeared.
Lights up on SQUEALER *and the* ANIMALS.

SQUEALER: Comrades! You do not imagine, I hope, that we pigs are taking the milk in a spirit of selfishness and privilege? Many of us actually dislike milk. I dislike it myself. Our sole object in mixing it in our mash is to preserve our health. Milk, — this has been proved by science, comrades — contains substances absolutely necessary to the well-being of pigs. We pigs are brain workers. The whole management and organisation of this farm depends on us. Day and night we are watching over your welfare. It is for *your* sake that we drink the milk.

BOXER: We never asked you to.

MURIEL: And it was never voted on at a meeting.

ALL: No!

MURIEL: Does Snowball know about this?

SQUEALER: Do you know what would happen if we pigs failed in our duty? Jones would come back! Yes, Jones would come back! Surely, comrades, surely there is no one who wants to see Jones back?
Consternation among the ANIMALS.

BOXER: None of us wants to see Jones back.

SHEEP: I propose the pigs be kept in good health.

ANIMALS (*voting*): Agreed! Agreed!

CLOVER: It's in our own interest.

BOXER: I propose that not only the milk, but the windfall apples when they come, and the maincrop of apples when they ripen, should be reserved for the pigs.

ALL (*voting*): Agreed! Agreed!

SQUEALER: Thank you, comrades.
Lights out.

BOY: How they toiled and sweated to get the hay in!
Lights up.

SQUEALER: Gee up, Boxer!
All the ANIMALS *freeze in horror.*

BOXER: Comrade Squealer, don't say that. You sound like a man.

SQUEALER: It may sound like that to you, comrade. But with our superior knowledge, it is natural that we pigs should direct the work and give the orders.
The ANIMALS *resume their work.*

BOY: It was the biggest harvest the farm had ever seen. There was no wastage. The hens and ducks with their sharp eyes gathered up the very last stalk. And not an animal on the farm had stolen so much as a mouthful. There was plenty to eat.
Lights down, except for the BOY.
All through that summer, the animals were happy, happy as they had never thought possible.
Lights up. The ANIMALS *are feeding in a long line.*

SHEEP: Now that the human beings have gone there is much more to eat.

CLOVER: The food tastes better, because it's *our* food. We grew it ourselves.

MURIEL: And it's not given to us by a mean and grudging master.
Lights down, except for the BOY.

BOY: Boxer was the admiration of everybody. He had one answer to every problem, every setback . . .
Lights up. BOXER *strikes an heroic pose.*

BOXER: I will work harder!

BOY: This was now his personal motto. It was much admired.
Lights down, except for the BOY.
Everyone worked according to his capability. Nobody stole, nobody grumbled, or almost nobody.
Lights up.

SQUEALER: Benjamin, aren't you happier without Jones?

BENJAMIN: In Jones' time, I used to work hard every day. Now he's gone and everything's changed. And I still work hard every day.

BOY: Nobody shirked. Or almost nobody.

SNOWBALL (*to* MOLLIE): Mollie, you were late again for work this morning.

SQUEALER: And you left work early this afternoon.

MOLLIE: There was another stone in my hoof.

ANIMALS (*snorting in contempt*): Huh!
Lights down, except for the BOY.

BOY: On Sundays there was no work. The day began at the flag pole.
Music. Lights up. MURIEL *hoists a flag on the flagstaff. It is a white hoof and horn on a green field.*

ALL THE ANIMALS: Our land was once a forest
　　　　　All green from shore to shore
　　　　　Till humans tore the greenwood down
　　　　　With axe and fire and saw.
　　　　　But see! The banners of the grass are raised!
　　　　　The trees are striding through the dawn!
　　　　　And the green flag is flying
　　　　　With the signs of hoof and horn.
　　　　　Yes, man is fleeing from the countryside
　　　　　And soon our meadows shall be clean,
　　　　　For the green flag is flying
　　　　　And all England shall be green.
　　　　　Shall be green, shall be green, shall be green.

SNOWBALL: The Hoof and Horn stand for the World Republic
　　　　　of the Animals which will be achieved when the human race
　　　　　has finally been overthrown.

ALL THE ANIMALS: Hooray!

SQUEALER: The meeting is now open.
　　　　　The ANIMALS *sit in a circle.*

SNOWBALL: We will first take the reports from the Animal
　　　　　Committees. Every Committee, comrades has exceeded
　　　　　expectation. Wherever I look, I see success. Particular praise
　　　　　is due to the hens, for their Egg Production Committee.

HENS: Thank you very much.

SNOWBALL: To the sheep, for their White Wool Movement.

SHEEP: Thaaanks!

SNOWBALL: And to the cows for their Clean Tails League.

COWS: Don't mention it.

NAPOLEON (*interrupting*): But I'm afraid we can't praise one
　　　　　Committee. I have to report the failure of the Wild
　　　　　Comrades Re-education Committee.

BENJAMIN: The what?

SQUEALER: The Wild Comrades Re-education Committee.

SNOWBALL: It is the best of my ideas. Its purpose is to tame
　　　　　the rats and the rabbits and the birds, and all the wild
　　　　　creatures.

CAT: It has provided a wonderful opportunity. I have done much
　　　　　good work on the sparrows.

ALL THE ANIMALS: Well done! Well done!

A HEN (*nervously*): I want to give a report on the Cat. She joined
the Re-education Committee and was very active in it for
some days. One day, I saw her sitting on the roof and
talking to some sparrows. They were just out of her reach.
She told them that as all animals are now equal, it was safe
to come and perch on her paw. But the sparrows didn't
believe her and kept their distance. Now the Cat no longer
comes to the Re-education Committee. I want to know
why, and I want to know now.
The HEN *and* CAT *confront each other, furious.*

NAPOLEON (*rescuing the situation*): Comrades! Snowball is a
brilliant pig. He inspires us all. But you can't expect that all
his ideas will succeed. Now I'm a practical pig, a pig of few
words. I believe that the future lies with the young. And I
believe that the education of the young is more important
than the re-education of anyone — wild or not. I have therefore made myself responsible for the education of the four
puppies. Mr Jones' puppies. We must take care of the
young.

ANIMALS (*voting*): Agreed! Agreed!

BOXER (*admiringly*): Napoleon is always right.

SNOWBALL: Napoleon *is* right. We must look after the young.
But what about the old? I'm worried about the old animals.
I propose that they be allowed to retire to a home of rest
in the orchard.

ANIMALS (*voting*): Agreed! Agreed!

NAPOLEON: But we can't do everything at once. We must be
practical. We need every able-bodied animal to work.

SNOWBALL: The old have earned some peace.

NAPOLEON: Peace? This is wartime. We're surrounded by
enemies. Everyone — old or young — must be trained in the
use of fire-arms.

SNOWBALL: No! That would be behaving like men. I will never
agree to that. Remember Old Major. We must never behave
like men. We must send out more and more pigeons to stir
up rebellion on other farms.
A silence.

NAPOLEON: If we cannot defend ourselves, we are bound to be
·conquered.

SNOWBALL: If rebellions happen everywhere, we shall have no
need to defend ourselves. I will not use a gun. You are

wrong, Comrade Napoleon.
A silence.
How will you vote? All of you? I want your opinions. Who
agrees with Napoleon? Who agrees with me? Boxer?

BOXER: I am thinking it over.

SNOWBALL: Benjamin? What do you think?

BENJAMIN: Not me. I'm not going to start thinking at my age.

SNOWBALL: Clover? Who do you think is right?

CLOVER: I cannot make up my mind. I always find myself in
agreement with the one who spoke last.

SNOWBALL: But you must be responsible. You must start
thinking for yourselves.
A silence.

NAPOLEON: Let us be practical.

SQUEALER: Yes! Let us go on with the meeting. Will you now
all rise for the report on the Reading and Writing classes.
All the ANIMALS *rise.*
All the pigs can now read and write perfectly. No further
work is necessary. I wish I could say the same for the rest
of the animals. Muriel reads fairly well, but is only
interested in reading from scraps of newspaper on the
rubbish dump, which she subsequently eats. It is suspected
that Benjamin can read as well as the pigs.

BENJAMIN: But as far as I know, there is nothing worth reading.

SQUEALER: Clover has learnt the whole alphabet, but cannot
put the words together. Boxer, however, is magnificent.
Boxer, will you repeat the alphabet?
With difficulty, BOXER *traces out the capitals on the floor.*

BOXER: Capital E . . . F . . . . . . G . . . . H . . . .
He stops, staring at the letters.

SQUEALER: You should be doing A, B, C, D, Boxer. You knew
those last week.
BOXER *looks mortified.*

BOXER: But this week, I have learnt capitals E, F, G, H . . .

SQUEALER: Yes, but now you have learnt capitals E, F, G, H,
you seem to have forgotten capitals A, B, C, D.

BOXER: It's too difficult. I think I shall have to be content with
the first four letters.

SQUEALER: Capitals A, B, C, D?

BOXER (*repeating slowly and carefully*): Yes. Capitals A, B, C,
    D. It's the best I can do, yes, the best. I will write them out
    once or twice every day to keep them fresh in my memory.
    So I hope it will be an example.

SQUEALER: And what about you, Mollie?

MOLLIE (*tracing the letters admiringly*): I know capitals M, and
    O. I know capital L and L; and capitals I and E.

SQUEALER: Don't you know any more letters?

MOLLIE: No. I only need to know the six letters which spell my
    name.

SQUEALER (*hiding his anger*): You must do better, Mollie. (*He
    screams.*) True Animalism cannot tolerate selfishness.

NAPOLEON: Order, Comrades, order! We must not get angry at
    meetings. We must always be reasonable.

SNOWBALL: Let us pass on to more serious matters. Some of
    our weaker comrades seem unable to learn the seven
    commandments by heart.

BOXER (*confessing*): Yes.

SNOWBALL: I have reduced the commandments to a single
    saying: 'Four Legs Good: Two Legs Bad'. This contains the
    essential principle of Animalism and whoever has
    thoroughly grasped it will be safe from human influences.

HEN: I object. I have only two legs. So have all birds.
    Protest breaks out among the BIRDS.

SNOWBALL (*silencing the din*): This is not so, comrades. A
    bird's wing is an organ of propulsion, not manipulation. It
    should therefore be regarded as a leg. Th distinguishing
    mark of Man is the *hand,* the instrument with which he
    does all his mischief.

HEN: I don't understand. Does that mean we are good?

SNOWBALL: Yes, you are good.

HEN: Good.

ANOTHER HEN: But I've still only got two legs.

SNOWBALL: It doesn't matter if you don't understand, as long
    as you accept my explanation. Do you accept my
    explanation?

ALL THE CHICKENS: Yes, we do. We accept your explanation.

SNOWBALL: So repeat after me please:
    Four legs good
    Two legs bad

The canon develops, sung by all the ANIMALS *as they learn the new maxim.*

ALL THE ANIMALS: **Four legs good**
Four legs good
Two legs bad
Two legs bad

The scene ends with the SHEEP *alone, still singing a joyful chorus. Having learnt it, they don't want to stop.*
Lights out.

BOY: The sheep enjoyed the song. They went on singing for fifteen minutes without stopping. Meanwhile Mr Jones was at the Red Lion every night complaining.
Lights up on the bar of the Red Lion. MR JONES *is talking to his neighbours.*

MR JONES: I think everybody should know — every man, every animal — the terrible wickedness that is now flourishing at Manor Farm. No, I won't call it 'Animal Farm'. They'd be starving if they didn't practise cannibalism. Do you know that they torture each other with red hot horse-shoes? Worst of all, they have their females in common . . .!
Lights out.

BOY: The other farmers were frightened by the rebellion at Animal Farm, and very anxious to stop their own animals hearing too much about it. But rumours of a wonderful farm — where the animals managed without human beings — continued to circulate. The pigs saw to that. They sent out flights of pigeons to mingle with the animals on neighbouring farms, tell them about the rebellion, and teach them the tune of 'Beasts of England'.
Lights up. The black figures manipulate flocks of pigeons on wires, swooping them round and round the stage. Meanwhile, 'Beasts of England' is heard in the distance. JONES *listens with two other* FARMERS.

JONES: How can the animals bring themselves to sing such contemptible rubbish! They need a good flogging.

BOY: And yet the song was irrepressible. The blackbirds whistled it in the hedges, the pigeons cooed it in the elms, it got into the din of the smithies and the tune of the church bells.
The sounds of the countryside are combined with 'Beasts of England'.

The human beings listened, and secretly trembled. For they
heard in the song a prophecy of their future doom.
The FARMERS *look frightened as the lights fade.*
Early in October, the animals met their next great test.
Lights up. The PIGEONS *bring a message to* SNOWBALL.
He listens to them.

SNOWBALL: Jones, Jones is coming!

BOY: The attack had long been expected, and everyone was
prepared. Snowball had studied an old book of Julius
Caesar's campaigns which he had found in the farmhouse.
He gave his orders quickly and in a couple of minutes,
every animal was at his post.
Martial music. JONES, *accompanied by the other*
FARMERS, *opens the five barred gate. He leads the posse
with a gun in his hands. The rest carry sticks.*

SNOWBALL (*an order*): Retreat, retreat!
The ANIMALS *turn and run into the barn. The* MEN *give
a shout of triumph.*

JONES: After them!
Once the MEN *are inside the barn, the* HORSES, *the*
COWS, *and the rest of the* PIGS *who are not in the barn
emerge from their hiding places and cut off their retreat.
Then the* MEN *are driven out of the barn.*

SNOWBALL: Charge!!
SNOWBALL *charges straight for* JONES. JONES *raises his
gun, and fires.* SNOWBALL *flattens himself for an instant
before resuming his charge, and behind him a* SHEEP *drops
dead.* SNOWBALL *charges* JONES' *legs.* JONES *is knocked
over and his gun flies out of his hands.*

ANIMALS: Hooray!
BOXER *rears on his hindlegs and strikes out with his great
ironshod hoofs. His first blow knocks a* STABLE LAD
lifeless. At the sight, the MEN *drop their sticks and start
running. Panic spreads. The* MEN *are gored, kicked, beaten,
trampled on. The* MEN *rush out of the yard, jump the gate,
and make a dash for the main road. All this is enacted in
great detail and accompanied by music.*
BOXER *paws with his hoof at the* STABLE LAD.

BOXER: He is dead. I didn't mean to do that. I forgot that I
was wearing iron shoes.

SNOWBALL: No sentimentality, comrade! War is war. The only

good human being is a dead human being!

BOXER: I don't want to take life. Not even human life.
    MURIEL *slowly pulls the flag up the flagpole. The*
    ANIMALS *lower their heads and sing 'The Green Flag'*
    quietly.

SQUEALER: But see the banners of the grass are raised,
    The trees are striding through the dawn.

    The STABLE LAD, *unobserved, comes round and runs off.*

NAPOLEON: Quickly! After him!

BOXER: No. Let him go. He was only a lad.
    There is an uneasy pause.

SQUEALER: Comrades, we must commemorate this great day.
    Medals must be awarded.

MURIEL: Medals?

SQUEALER: I suggest 'Animal Hero First Class'.

NAPOLEON: I propose that Boxer be named 'Animal Hero,
    First Class'.

ALL THE ANIMALS (*voting*): Agreed!

MURIEL: Give Snowball a medal too.
    The ANIMALS *look nervously at the dead* SHEEP.

SNOWBALL: Our dear comrade here is also a hero. But alas, he
    is a dead hero.

SQUEALER: Let us confer a decoration posthumously on him:
    'Animal Hero, Second Class'.

ALL THE ANIMALS (*voting*): Agreed! Agreed!
    MOLLIE *enters from the stables.*

MOLLIE: Have they all gone?

SQUEALER: Yes.

MOLLIE: Is it safe?

SNOWBALL: Yes.

MOLLIE: I am sorry I couldn't stay. I had to hide my head in
    the hay. I can't stand explosions.
    The ANIMALS *all look at her.*

SQUEALER: Comrades, what shall we call this glorious day.
    Every October the twelfth, every anniversary we shall have
    a celebration. And what shall the battle be called?

BOXER: There is only one name for the battle: Snowball's
    Battle.

NAPOLEON (*very quickly*): No. I think you will agree that that
is the wrong name. You all fought this battle. You all
brought us victory. Let it be named the Battle of the
Cowshed. That was after all the place — the place where the
ambush was sprung.

ALL THE ANIMALS: Agreed! Agreed!
NAPOLEON *and* SNOWBALL *look at each other.*
Lights down.

BOY: Now Winter drew on. . . .
Lights up. MOLLIE *and* CLOVER *are together.*

CLOVER: Mollie, I have something very serious to say to you.
This morning I saw you looking over the hedge that divides
Animal Farm form Mr Pilkington's farm. Mr Pilkington was
standing on the other side of the hedge. And — I was a
long way away, but I am almost certain I saw this — he was
talking to you, and you were allowing him to stroke your
nose. What does that mean Mollie?

MOLLIE: He didn't! I wasn't! It isn't true. . . . (*She begins to
paw the ground.*)

CLOVER: Mollie: Look me in the face. Do you give me your
word of honour that Mr Pilkington was not stroking your
nose?

MOLLIE: How dare you ask me such questions?
MOLLIE *takes to her heels and gallops away. The lights
fade.*

BOY: Three days later, Mollie disappeared.
Lights up on all the ANIMALS *at the meeting.*

FIRST PIGEON: We have seen Mollie on the other side of the
village. She wasbetween the shafts of a smart dogcart
painted red and black.
A vision of MOLLIE *appears trotting in an idyllic dappled
light. She is covered with ribbons and is led by*
MR PILKINGTON *who bears a whip. The* ANIMALS *stare
in disbelief.*

SECOND PIGEON: Mr Pilkington was stroking her nose and
feeding her sugar.
MOLLIE *sings as she trots.*

MOLLIE: **Twenty-seven ribbons**
Twenty-seven ribbons
Sugar lumps for Mollie
A kindly blacksmith

And a gentle vet.
Master brought my ribbons
And my shiny brasses —
Give the humans what they want
And that is what you'll get.

And the wheels flow around
With a whirring, purring sound
As I step along Speedwell Lane,
And I hurry home to the curry-comb
With twenty-seven multi-coloured ribbons in my mane.

Twenty-seven ribbons
Sugar lumps for Mollie
A careful grooming
After every trip.
I have heard some horses
Say that Man is cruel —
But if you're obedient
You'll seldom feel the whip.

Yes the wheels flow around
With a whirring, purring sound
As I step along Speedwell Lane,
And I hurry home
To the curry-comb
With twenty-seven multi-coloured ribbons in my mane.
Twenty-seven ribbons
Twenty-seven ribbons
Twenty-seven ribbons in my mane.

MOLLIE *disappears.*
Lights down.

BOY: None of the animals ever mentioned Mollie again.
Lights up in the barn on all the ANIMALS.
By custom, it was now expected that the pigs should decide
all questions of farm policy. But their decisions still had to
be ratified by a majority vote. This arrangement would have
worked well enough if it had not been for the continual
disputes between Snowball and Napoleon.

SNOWBALL: I propose that we sew a bigger acreage with barley!

The ANIMALS *shout agreement and disagreement after
each proposition. It is a very noisy meeting.*

NAPOLEON: I propose that we sow a bigger acreage with oats!

SNOWBALL: The big Copse Meadow is just right for cabbages!

NAPOLEON: The meadow is useless for anything except roots!
Uproar from the ANIMALS.

SNOWBALL: Comrades! Comrades!

BOY: At the meetings, Snowball often won over the majority by
his brilliant speeches. . . .

SNOWBALL: **Yesterday had the smell of blood,**
Slavery, loss and pain.
Today is sweaty with constant work
And I know that you feel the strain.
But tomorrow, tomorrow is your children's day
And we labour so they may gain
The potatoes and apples and barley of the future
With its deep green meadows
And its towering golden grain —
Tomorrow.

ALL THE ANIMALS: Tomorrow!

SNOWBALL: We spend too much time, comrades, carting dung.
MURIEL *enters carrying a child's blackboard in her teeth.*
On it there is a map of the fields drawn in chalk.

I ask you to support this scheme. Here is a map of the farm.
Each animal is given a starting point, he moves three steps
a day. If all animals drop their dung directly in the field,
and at a different spot each day, the saving of labour in
carting will . . .

NAPOLEON: May I interrupt? I have no schemes, I believe in
quiet, conscientious work, not risks.

BOY: Napoleon was better at canvassing support for himself
between the meetings. He was especially successful with the
sheep, who were always ready to interrupt when Snowball's
scheme sounded too difficult.

NAPOLEON: Snowball's scheme may be very ingenious, but it
won't work.

SNOWBALL: Yes, it will work!

THE SHEEP (*a raucous interruption*):

Four legs good
Four legs good
Two legs bad
Two legs bad

BOXER (*silencing them*): Now then, now then! The sheep must allow us to talk. We must say what we think.
NAPOLEON turns and looks at BOXER and smiles.

NAPOLEON: Of course, Boxer.
Lights fade.

BOY: But of all their controversies, the most bitter was the one over the windmill — the windmill designed by Snowball.
A large sheet of paper has been pinned over the barn entrance. On it, is a rough working drawing of a windmill. The ANIMALS examine it with excitement and interest. SNOWBALL is not there. NAPOLEON looks at the drawing, sniffs it, and then lifts his leg and urinates on it. The ANIMALS gasp.

NAPOLEON (*calling*): Snowball!

SNOWBALL (*entering*): I'm here, comrade.

NAPOLEON: This windmill of yours is impossible.

SNOWBALL: Diffcult, comrade, not impossible. We will have to gather stone for its walls, we will have to make sails, we will have to buy dynamos. I believe all this can be accomplished in one year.

NAPOLEON: One year!

SNOWBALL: It will supply our farm with electrical power.

NAPOLEON: But we can't do everything at once! Why can't you be realistic?
NAPOLEON stares at SNOWBALL.
The rest of the ANIMALS are uneasy.

SNOWBALL: I *am* being realistic. This power will do your work for you. You can graze at your ease in the fields or improve your minds with reading and conversations. So much labour will be saved that you animals will only need to work three days a week.

MURIEL (*admiringly*): Snowball, how did you think of this?

SNOWBALL: Mr Jones left an excellent book behind: *A Thousand Useful Things to do About the House*. It has taught me how to lay bricks and to understand electricity. So now I can build windmills!

BOXER: Put it to the vote! Put it to the vote!

NAPOLEON: We'll be past voting, comrades, when our stomachs are empty. I'm a plain pig, a practical pig, and I say this. The great need at the moment is to increase food production. If we waste time on windmills, we'll starve to death.

SNOWBALL: Do you deny my ideas?

NAPOLEON (*suddenly shouting*): Yes, I deny your ideas.

BOY: The animals were furious. War was near. They no longer wanted to argue; they wanted to fight.
The ANIMALS *divide into two factions on opposite sides of the stage and confront each other.*

FIRST FACTION: **A vote for Snowball means food for the future!**

SECOND FACTION: **Vote for Napoleon and eat it now!**

FIRST FACTION: **A vote for Snowball means food for the future!**

SECOND FACTION: **Vote for Napoleon and eat it now!**
SNOWBALL*'s voice rises above the din.*

SNOWBALL: Think, comrades, how life can be on Animal Farm when sordid labour is lifted from our back. I am thinking far beyond chaff-cutters and turnip-slicers. Electricity can do many things. It can operate threshing machines, ploughs and harrows, rollers and reapers. And it can supply every stall with its own electric light, its own hot and cold water, *and* an electric heater.
As SNOWBALL *speaks, the* ANIMALS *in* NAPOLEON*'s faction change their minds and go over to* SNOWBALL*'s. Only the* PIGS *remain.*
Think of the future. Think of your children. Think of the dignity of animals when they are freed from toil. Do you vote for the windmill?

ALL THE ANIMALS: Yes, we do. We vote for the windmill.
Suddenly NAPOLEON *utters a high-pitched blood-curdling scream. There is a loud noise of dogs baying and the silhouettes of two enormous black* DOGS *appear in the barn behind the drawing of the windmill. With a yelp, they tear down the drawing and attack* SNOWBALL. *He confronts them for a moment in terror, and then runs away through the gate and out of the farm. He is pursued by the* DOGS.
The ANIMALS *are terrified. They watch as* SNOWBALL *is chased away into the distance.*
Silence.

BOXER: Snowball's gone.

CLOVER: Gone?

SQUEALER: Yes, gone, gone back to the world of men where he belongs. Snowball, who we now see, was little better than a traitor and a coward.

BOXER (*emphatically*): He wasn't.

CLOVER: He fought bravely at the Battle of the Cowshed.

SQUEALER: Only the guilty run away. And I believe the time will come when we shall discover that Snowball's part in the battle was much exaggerated. Do you still support Snowball, comrades? Snowball with his moonshine of windmills?
The DOGS *come bounding back and surround* NAPOLEON, *asking for approval.*

BOXER: Where do those dogs come from?

NAPOLEON: They are my puppies. I've brought them up to be big dogs.

BENJAMIN: They wag their tails at you just as their parents wagged their tails at Mr Jones.

NAPOLEON: That's right, Benjamin. They are well trained. . . . From now on the Sunday morning debates are cancelled. They are unnecessary and waste time. In future, all questions relating to the working of the farm will be settled by a special committee of pigs, presided over by me. We shall meet in private, and afterwards communicate our decisions to the rest of you. All you animals will still assemble on Sunday morning to sing 'The Green Flag' and of course to receive your orders for the week. But there will be no more debates.

MURIEL: No more debates?

CLOVER (*tentatively*): If there's no debate, there's no Animal Farm.

BOXER: Shan't we vote any more?

NAPOLEON: No, Boxer. But your wishes will be carefully considered by the special committee of the pigs. We live in dangerous times. We must show solidarity and have strong leadership. We must defend ourselves from our enemies.

SQUEALER: I'm sure Comrade Napoleon would be only too happy to let you make your own decisions by yourselves, but sometimes you might make the wrong decisions and then where should we be?

BOXER: That's right.

SQUEALER: Discipline, comrades, iron discipline, that is the watch-word for today. One false step, and our enemies will be upon us. Surely, comrades, you don't want Jones back?

BOY: Once again, this argument was unanswerable.

ANIMALS: No. We don't want Jones back.

BENJAMIN: But why can't we vote?

SQUEALER: Comrades. I trust every animal here appreciates the sacrifice that Comrade Napoleon has made in taking this extra labour upon himself. Do not imagine, comrades, that leadership is pleasure! On the contrary, it is a deep and heavy responsibility.

MURIEL: If having debates on Sunday mornings will bring Jones back, then the debates must stop.

SQUEALER: Perhaps the farmers will get to hear of our disagreements and think we are weak.

BOXER (*his mind made up*): Comrades. I have now had time to think things over and I think I have a solution. What Comrade Napoleon is offering us is leadership. He is a practical pig, a pig of few words. Let's do what he says. (*Pause.*) Agreed?

ALL THE ANIMALS (*voting*): Agreed! Agreed!

NAPOLEON: Thank you, comrades.

NAPOLEON *and the* PIGS *leave. There is a long silence. The* ANIMALS *look at* BOXER.

BOXER (*reassuringly*): We have chosen wisely, comrades. Napoleon is always right. **Long Live Animal Farm!**

ALL THE ANIMALS: **Long Live Animal Farm!**

ACT TWO

The ANIMALS *are seen in a long line, waiting to pay their respects to the skull of* OLD MAJOR, *which is now nailed to the telegraph pole.*

BOY: Every Sunday morning at ten o'clock, the animals assembled to pay their respects to Old Major. His skull, now clean of flesh, had been disinterred from the orchard and nailed to a telegraph pole.

SQUEALER: And now Minimus, the first Animalist poet, will pay his tribute to Old Major.

MINIMUS: Once all us animals' eyes were blind
To the fact of our slavery.
Old Major had a very clever mind,
He showed us Man's knavery.

Old Major
Please feed us!
Help us win our daily war.
Old Major
Please lead us!
Thank you very much, great boar!

So let us salute the skull of Major then.
O behold his enormous brains!
And every Sunday when the clock strikes ten
We'll march past his remains.

NAPOLEON: I have a brief announcement, comrades. We must look to the future. Animalism will lead us to incredible achievements. No task is too great for Animalism. *We're going to build a windmill!*

ALL THE ANIMALS: What?

NAPOLEON: The special committee of pigs expects that the building of the windmill will take two years.
NAPOLEON *leaves.*

BOXER: But I thought that Napoleon thought that the windmill . .?

SQUEALER: Napoleon was never actually opposed to the windmill. The plan which Snowball drew was copied from some papers stolen from Napoleon. The windmill is actually Napoleon's own creation. And it always was.

BENJAMIN:Then why did he speak so strongly against it?

SQUEALER: That was Comrade Napoleon's cunning. He seemed to oppose the windmill simply as manoeuvre to get rid of Snowball. This is something called tactics. Napoleon is expert at tactics.

MURIEL: But why did he want to get rid of Snowball?

SQUEALER: Because he was not practical, comrades, not realistic. He went too fast. I suppose you could say he was leading us quickly to starvation. The windmill will prevent that.

BOXER (*his mind made up*): If Comrade Napoleon says we need a windmill, then we must build a windmill. Agreed?

ALL THE ANIMALS (*voting*): Agreed! Agreed!

SQUEALER: Thank you, comrades.

BOY: But the windmill proved difficult, because there were no stones on the farm. There were some huge boulders on top of a cliff. But the problem was how to break the boulders into pieces the right size. After weeks of thought . . .

SQUEALER (*an inspiration*): Ah!

BOY: The pigs had an idea.

SQUEALER: We will shove these huge boulders over the edge of the cliff. We will smash them by using the force of gravity. *Lights up. Music.*
    BOXER *is seen trying to push the boulder. During the song the other* ANIMALS *come and help him.*

BOXER: **There was a whacking great limestone boulder**
    Must've weighed near a ton.
    I tried to shift it with my shoulder —
    Ugh! (*Shoving.*)

    — Couldn't be done.
    So I called a passing comrade over
    And she came at the run.

BOXER *and* CLOVER: **We tried to move that limestone boulder**
    Ugh! (*Shoving.*)

    — Couldn't be done.

    We appealed to the Sheep Committee
    Called up the Goats' Brigade
    And the chickens and the geese to shift that rock —
    Ugh! (*Shoving.*)

ALL ANIMALS: **— But it just stayed.**

It just stayed where it was
That great lump of stone
And all of the beasts
Gave a mighty moan
We'll never shift it!
The rock's too big!

SQUEALER: Give it one more try

MINIMUS: Says a stout-hearted pig!

ALL THE ANIMALS: So we gave one more shove
And we gave one more lift
And that whacking great boulder
Started to shift
And we gave it a shove
With all our heart and soul
And that whacking great boulder
Started to roll — and roll — and roll and —

The ANIMALS *pause as they watch the boulder roll over the edge. There is a huge crash.*

ALL THE ANIMALS:
There was a whacking great limestone boulder
But the animals worked as one
Yes, through animal co-operation
Anything can be done!
Anything can be done!
Anything can be done!

CLOVER: Boxer! Don't over-strain yourself.

BOXER: We're not getting enough food. I'll pick up when the spring grass comes on.

CLOVER: I am worried about you, Boxer. You think there are two answers to every problem: 'I will work harder'; or 'Napoleon is always right'.

BOXER: They *are* the answers.
Lights down.

BOY: All that year the animals worked like slaves to till the fields. They also worked to build the windmill.
Lights up. The ANIMALS *are seen building the windmill.*
But they were happy in their work. Everything they did was for their own benefit and for those who would come after them, not for a pack of idle, thieving human beings.

NAPOLEON (*entering*): Comrades, in future there will be work

on Sunday afternoons. This work is of course strictly
voluntary. But any animal who absents himself from it
must expect to have his rations reduced by half.
Furthermore, I have decided on a new policy. From now
on, Animal Farm will engage in trade with neighbouring
farms.

MURIEL: Comrade Napoleon, will you repeat that?

NAPOLEON: Animal Farm will engage in trade with
neighbouring farms!
The ANIMALS *gasp in amazement. The* DOGS *growl.*
This is, of course, not for any commercial purpose. We need
money to buy the materials which are urgently necessary —
tools, paraffin oil, string. And dog biscuits. I am therefore
making arrangements to sell a stack of hay and part of our
current wheat crop. If we need more money later, to buy
a dynamo for the windmill for instance, it will have to be
obtained by the sale of eggs. There is always a market for
eggs in the village.
The HENS *cluck in protest.*

HEN: What! What! What about our chicks?
The DOGS *growl.*

NAPOLEON: The hens should welcome this sacrifice as their own
special contribution towards the building of the windmill.
The ANIMALS *are uneasy. Two young* PIGS *come forward.*

FIRST PIG: Comrade Leader, we represent the younger pigs and
we must object. These were among the earliest resolutions
passed after Jones was expelled.

SECOND PIG: One:

FIRST PIG: Never to have any dealings with human beings.

SECOND PIG: Two:

THIRD PIG: Never to engage in trade.

SECOND PIG: Three:

FIRST PIG: Never to make use of money.

SQUEALER: Are you certain this isn't something you have
dreamed, comrade? Have you any record of these
resolutions? Are they written down anywhere?

BENJAMIN: I remember them.

CLOVER: We all remember them.

BOXER: Comrade Snowball always told us not to behave like
men.

ALL THE ANIMALS: Yes, that's right.

THE SHEEP (*interrupting*): **Four legs good**
    Four legs good
    Two legs bad
    Two legs bad
    NAPOLEON *raises his trotter for silence.*

NAPOLEON: There is no need for any further discussion. I have recognised necessity. We need money — so we will engage in trade. I have made all the arrangements. There will be no need for any of you animals to come into contact with human beings — that would clearly be most undesirable. I shall do that myself. Mr Whymper, a solicitor living in the village, has agreed to act as the agent between Animal Farm and the outside world. He will visit the farm every Monday morning to receive his instructions.
An uneasy silence.
Long live Animal Farm!

ALL THE ANIMALS: Long live Animal Farm.
A bicycle bell is heard ringing.

BOY: Every Monday, Mr Whymper visited the farm.
MR WHYMPER *rides in on a bicycle, dismounts and shakes hands with* NAPOLEON.
The animals watched him with dread. Nevertheless, the sight of Napoleon on all fours, delivering orders to Whymper, who stood on two legs, roused their pride and partly reconciled them to the new arrangement.

NAPOLEON: Do I make myself clear?

MR WHYMPER: Perfectly, Mr Napoleon.
MR WHYMPER *hands a cheque to* NAPOLEON.

NAPOLEON: Cheques are no use to me. I need five pound notes.
The ANIMALS *watch in delight as* MR WHYMPER *counts out the five pound notes.*

MR WHYMPER: One, Two, Three, Four, Five, Six, Seven, Eight, Nine, Ten.

NAPOLEON: That makes fifty pounds.

ANIMALS (*in wonder*): Fifty pounds!

NAPOLEON: Thank you, Mr Whymper.

MR WHYMPER: It's been a real pleasure, Mr Napoleon.
NAPOLEON *and the* ANIMALS *watch* MR WHYMPER *ride off on his bicycle. Suddenly* NAPOLEON *leads all the* PIGS *into the farmhouse at a fast trot.*

BOY: It was about this time that the pigs suddenly moved into the farmhouse.

BOXER: Why are they going in there?

SQUEALER (*at the farmhouse door*): It is absolutely necessary that the pigs, who are after all the brains of the farm, should have a quiet place to work in. It is also more suited to the dignity of the Leader to live in a house than a mere sty.
He leaves. The lights change.

FIRST SHEEP (*gossiping*): I hear that the pigs take their meals in the kitchen.

SECOND SHEEP: And use the drawing room to play in.

THIRD SHEEP: And sleep in the beds.

FOURTH SHEEP: Never!

BOXER (*keeping order*): Napoleon is always right.

CLOVER: I remember a definite ruling against beds.
MURIEL and CLOVER go over to the barn and look at the seven commandments on the wall.

CLOVER: Muriel, read me the fourth commandment.

MURIEL (*reading with some difficulty*): It says: 'Animals shall never sleep in beds with sheets on'.

CLOVER: I don't remember the fourth commandment mentioning sheets.

MURIEL: But it must have done. It's there on the wall.
SQUEALER looks out of the upstairs window of the farmhouse.

SQUEALER: Comrades! You did not suppose, surely comrade, that there was ever a ruling against *beds*? A bed merely means a place to sleep in. A pile of straw in a stall is a bed, properly regarded. The rule was against *sheets,* which are a human invention. We have removed the sheets from the farmhouse beds and sleep between blankets. And very comfortable blankets they are too.
Lights down.

BOY: By the autumn, the animals were tired but happy. They had had a hard year and after selling part of the hay and corn to Mr Whymper, they were still hungry. But the windmill compensated for everything.
Music. Lights up on all the ANIMALS building the windmill, block by block.

BOXER: We are working harder. We are building our windmill.

ALL THE ANIMALS: Hooray!

BOY: Only Old Benjamin refused to grow enthusiastic.

BENJAMIN: Huh! Windmills! Electricity! The more you have
the more you want. God has given me a tail to keep the
flies off. But I'd sooner have no tail and no flies.
The lights change. It is winter. Snow falls. The ANIMALS
huddle in a group.

BOY: In January food fell short. For days at a time, the animals
had nothing to eat but chaff and mangels.

ALL THE ANIMALS: Food! Where's our food? Give us food!

CLOVER: Have you heard what the pigeons are saying? When
we're really weak, Jones intends to bring twenty men
against us all armed with guns.

BOY: Starvation stared them in the face. But it was vitally
necessary to hide this face from the outside world.
The lights change. NAPOLEON *and* MR WHYMPER *enter
from the barn.* MR WHYMPER *is once more counting
out the money.*

MR WHYMPER: One, two, three, four, five, six, seven, eight,
nine, ten. Another fifty pounds for your very fine grain,
Mr Napoleon.

NAPOLEON: Thank you, Mr Whymper.

MR WHYMPER: I hear rumours in the village that you're running
short of food.

NAPOLEON: Not so, Mr Whymper.

MR WHYMPER: Won't you sell me some more grain then, Mr
Napoleon?

NAPOLEON: No. The animals must be fed, and fed well.
Goodbye, Mr Whymper.

MR WHYMPER: Very well. Cheerio, Mr Napoleon.
MR WHYMPER *rides off on his bicycle.*

BOY: Mr Whymper has been nicely fooled. The grain bins had
been filled at Napoleon's order with sand, which was then
covered with what was left of the grain. In fact, the animals
were desperately hungry.
Lights up on the Sunday morning meeting. NAPOLEON
is absent. SQUEALER *is speaking.*

SQUEALER: Comrades. We need grain. Napoleon has therefore
decreed that the hens must surrender their eggs.

HENS (*screaming in protest*): What?
> *High up on a rafter, all the* HENS *appear. They are sitting out of reach.*

SQUEALER: He has accepted, through the good offices of Whymper, a contract for four hundred eggs a week. The price of these will pay for enough grain and meal to give us food until Summer.

FIRST HEN: But the clutches are ready for the spring sitting.

SECOND HEN: It's murder if you take the eggs away now.

BOY: And for the first time since the expulsion of Jones, there was something resembling a rebellion.

HENS: We can't spare the eggs.

SQUEALER: You must do your duty?

HENS: We can't spare the eggs.
> Can't you see we're broody?

SQUEALER: We must have the eggs
> We must pay our way now.

HENS: It's murder, yes murder
> To take our eggs away now.

SQUEALER: Consider economics —
> The eggs have got to go.

HENS: Consider our unborn chicks.

SQUEALER: We must have the eggs.

HENS: No! No!
> Till each egg has the right
> To become a hen
> There'll be no more eggs
> To be sold to men,
> There'll be no eggs at all.
> Let the eggs rain down
> From the henhouse sky.

The HENS *drop their eggs onto the* ANIMALS *below them.*

> Let the egg yolks dry.
> Till each egg has the right
> To become a hen
> There'll be no more eggs
> To be sold to men.
> There'll be no eggs at all.

NAPOLEON (*entering*): Our feathered comrades, it appears,
> Have lost all sense of reason

> And their reactionary acts
> Are tantamount to treason
>
> To turn them back to sanity
> And save them from self slaughter
> I order that the hens shall be
> Deprived of food and water

BOY: For five days the hens held out.

HENS (*weakening*): **Till each egg has the right**
> **To become a hen**
> **There'll be no eggs at all.**
> **Let the eggs rain down**
> **From the henhouse sky.**
>
> *The* HENS *fall dead off the rafters, one by one.*
>
> Let the eggshells smash
> Let the good yolks dry.
>
> *Lights down.*

BOY: Finally, they capitulated and went back to their nesting boxes. Nine hens had died. (*A small toy van crosses the stage to the gate and stops.*) From now on, a grocer's van drove up to the farm once a week to take the eggs away. And once a week the animals watched them go. But they still had no more to eat. (*The van leaves the stage.*) There was secret whispering in the night, a whispering that Napoleon, like Snowball, was soon to be chased away. Who was to chase him? Where was Mr Whymper's money going? Why was there no food? Morale was very low. Napoleon knew that he had to do something.

NAPOLEON: Comrades, I have alarming news. Snowball is secretly frequenting the farm by night!
> *The* ANIMALS *quickly grow hysterical with fear.*
> He has stolen the corn, upset the milk, broken the eggs, trampled the seedbeds, gnawed the bark off the fruit trees. Did you notice that window that was broken last week? Did you notice the drain of the cowshed? It was blocked up. I will go further. I believe that the lost key of the storeshed was filched by Snowball and thrown down the well! Any animal who can give evidence of Snowball's villanies will be rewarded with extra rations.

ALL THE ANIMALS: Extra rations!
> *Two* COWS *come forward.*

COWS: We have a unanimous statement to make. Snowball has
    crept into our stall and milked us in our sleep. All of us.
    Yes, all of us.

NAPOLEON: There must obviously be a full investigation into
    Snowball's activities. (*Giving several deep sniffs.*) Snowball!
    He has been here! I can smell him distinctly!
    The DOGS *let out bloodcurdling growls.* NAPOLEON
    leaves accompanied by his DOGS. *The* ANIMALS *are very
    alarmed.*

BOY: The animals were thoroughly frightened. It seemed to them
    that Snowball was an invisible influence who was
    everywhere.
    SQUEALER *enters suddenly. The* ANIMALS *jump with
    fear.*

SQUEALER: Comrades! The most terrible thing has been
    discovered. We had thought that Snowball's opposition to
    Comrade Napoleon was caused by his vanity and ambition.
    But we were wrong, comrades. Snowball was in league with
    Jones from the very start. He was Jones' secret agent all the
    time. This has been proved by documents which have only
    just been discovered. To my mind, this explains a great
    deal, comrades. Did we not see for ourselves how he
    attempted to get us defeated and destroyed at the Battle of
    the Cowshed!
    There is a stunned silence.

BOXER: He didn't. Snowball fought bravely at the Battle of the
    Cowshed. I saw him myself.

MURIEL: We made him Animal Hero, First Class, immediately
    afterwards.

SQUEALER: That was our mistake, comrades. For we now know
    that in reality he was trying to lure us to our doom. Do you
    not remember how Snowball suddenly turned and fled,
    and many animals followed him? Surely you remember
    that, comrades?
    The ANIMALS *are confused.*

CLOVER: I remember that Snoball turned and retreated.

MURIEL: But that was his tactics. Military tactics.

BOXER: Comrade Squealer, I do not believe that Comrade
    Snowball was a traitor at the beginning. What he has done
    since is different. But I believe that at the Battle of the
    Cowshed, he was a good comrade.

SQUEALER: Our Leader, Comrade Napoleon, has stated
  categorically — *categorically,* comrades — that Snowball
  was Jones' agent from the very beginning. Yes, and from
  long before the rebellion was ever thought of!
  A long pause. The ANIMALS *look confused. They watch*
  BOXER.

BOXER: Comrade Napoleon says that?

SQUEALER: Yes, he does.

BOXER: Then that is different. If Comrade Napoleon says it, it
  must be right.

SQUEALER (*delighted*): There you are, comrades! There you see
  the true spirit of Animalism!
  There is a roar of rage from NAPOLEON. *He appears at
  the window of the farmhouse.*

NAPOLEON: Comrades! We have been robbed! When I capture
  Whymper, he shall be boiled in oil and then torn apart by
  every pig on the farm. The five pound notes are forgeries.
  Whymper has got the eggs for nothing! Death to Whymper!

ALL THE ANIMALS (*hysterical again*): Death to Whymper!
  Death to Whymper!

SQUEALER: Let me give you a warning. Every animal on this
  farm must keep his eyes very wide open. We know that
  some of you are Snowball's secret agents. We know you
  are! We have sniffed you out. And we will hunt you down.
  The ANIMALS *look uneasily at each other as the lights
  fade.*

BOY: Four days later, Napoleon ordered all the animals to
  assemble.
  Lights up. Enter NAPOLEON *and* SQUEALER.

NAPOLEON: Comrades. There is a terrible threat to our future.
  There are traitors here on Animal Farm. The traitors must
  be brought to justice.

SQUEALER: Bring them before us. Let the trials commence.
  Two young PIGS *enter to be tried.*

FIRST PIG: We represent the younger pigs.

NAPOLEON: Confess your crimes.
  A silence.

FIRST PIG: What?

NAPOLEON: Confess your crimes!

FIRST PIG (*anxiously starting to play his part*): Oh yes, we have been secretly in touch with Snowball.

SECOND PIG: Ever since his expulsion.

FIRST PIG: We collaborated with him.

SECOND PIG: And we have entered into an agreement with him to hand over Animal Farm to Mr Jones.

NAPOLEON: What has Snowball admitted to you?

FIRST PIG: That he has been Jones' secret agent for many years.
NAPOLEON shrieks. The barn doors open and the DOGS begin to drag the PIGS inside.

NAPOLEON: It saddens me that the younger pigs should be guilty of such treason.

FIRST PIG: You told us . . . We would live . . . If we confessed!
The doors shut on the PIGS. They shriek as they are bitten to death. NAPOLEON looks at the ANIMALS.

NAPOLEON: Has any other animal anything to confess?
Two HENS enter to be tried.

SQUEALER: Confess!

FIRST HEN: Snowball appeared to me in a dream and incited me to disobey Napoleon's orders.

SECOND HEN: We led the rebellion over the eggs. We fully confess our faults.
NAPOLEON shrieks. The HENS are dragged into the barn and killed.
A silence.
A BULL comes forward nervously to be tried.

SQUEALER: Next! Confess!

BULL: I confess to having hidden six turnips during last year's harvest. I have eaten them one by one in secret. Night after night.
NAPOLEON shrieks. The BULL is dragged into the barn and killed.
Lights down.

BOY: The air was heavy with the smell of blood — unknown since the days of Jones. But this seemed far worse. Until today, no animal had killed another animal. Not even a rat had been killed.
Lights up. The ANIMALS are standing round a big pool of blood on the floor. A long pause.

CLOVER: What are you going to do, Boxer?

BOXER: I do not understand it. I would not have believed it.
The only solution, as I see it, is to work harder. From now
on, I shall get up a full hour earlier in the mornings. And
work.
BOXER *leaves*.

ALL THE ANIMALS: Say what you think
But the best thing to think
Is nothing —
That's excellent thinking.

Eat what you like
But the best food to like
Is nothing —
It's not on the ration.

Do what you want
But the best thing to do
Is nothing —
And mind how you do it.

Go where you want
But the place to go
Is nowhere —
You might get permission.

Obey them.
When they tell you what to do.
You are nothing.
Nothing.

Believe them
When they tell you what is true.
You're nothing.
Nothing.

Keep your nose to the grindstone
And your shoulder to the wheel.
Listen
When they tell you what to feel
And —

Feel what you like
But the best thing to feel
Is nothing

(*Whispering*:)
Nothing.

CLOVER, BENJAMIN *and* MURIEL *are by the barn.*

CLOVER: Read the sixth commandment please, Benjamin.

BENJAMIN: I refuse to meddle in such matters.

CLOVER: Will you read it, Muriel?

MURIEL: 'Animals shall never kill animals without good cause'.

CLOVER: I don't remember those last three words, 'without good cause'.

MURIEL: The commandment has not been violated. There was good reason to kill any animal who helped Snowball.

CLOVER (*with determination*): We must start again. We must try to remember what Old Major said and start again.
Beasts of England, Beasts of Ireland
Beasts of land and sea and skies.

SQUEALER: Comrades, by a special decree of Comrade Napoleon, 'Beasts of England' has been abolished. From now on it is forbidden to sing it.

CLOVER: Why?

SQUEALER: It is no longer needed, comrade, that's why. 'Beasts of England' expressed our longing for a better society in the days to come. But now the days to come have come. That society has been established. Clearly the song no longer has any purpose.

CLOVER: Do you agree? I want to know.

MURIEL: Yes.
Lights change. MINIMUS *is singing the new anthem.*

MINIMUS: **But see! The trotters of the pigs are raised!**
The swine advance with bellies stout!
And the green flag is flying
With the curly tail and snout!
Yes, pigs are leading all the animals.
Oh, follow them, nor reason why,
For the green flag is flying
And all England is our sty
Is our sty, is our sty, is our sty!

BOXER: Somehow or other, that song doesn't seem to come up to 'Beasts of —

ALL THE ANIMALS: Sshh!!

BOXER: — To what we used to sing.
Lights fade.

BOY: As the summer wore on, the rumours of an impending attack grew stronger and stronger. It was harvest time. It was inexplicable that there was no food. It was also inexplicable that Mr Whymper was visiting the farm again. In fact, all the grain was being secretly sold to him for ready cash so that the pigs could buy whisky.
Lights up. SQUEALER *dances in and addresses the* ANIMALS.

SQUEALER: **Animalism is a complicated business**
Inflexible equality is unrealistic
Our systems successful, though with
Certain contradictions
The proof is in the pudding
Let me quote you statistics.
The production of every class of foodstuff has increased. Some by two hundred percent, some by three hundred percent, some by five hundred percent. As the case might be. Isn't this a great achivement?

BENJAMIN: We're still hungry.

SQUEALER: What? Speak up Benjamin. Let us hear your thoughts.

BENJAMIN: I have no thoughts.

SQUEALER: Then look happy. Do you never laugh, Benjamin?

BENJAMIN: I see nothing to laugh about.

SQUEALER: But we want you to laugh, Benjamin. All of us. Come on. Laugh!
The DOGS *growl.* BENJAMIN *begins to laugh, his hysteria mounting until he is completely out of control. The other* ANIMALS *gather round him in sympathy. He stops, broken.*

SQUEALER: Next time, Benjamin, laugh when I tell you to.
Lights down.

BOY: In September, by a tremendous effort — the windmill was finished.
Lights up on the finished windmill. BOXER *pushes the sails and they start to turn.*

ALL THE ANIMALS: Hooray!

NAPOLEON: May I personally congratulate each and every animal on this achievement. The mill will be called 'Napoleon Mill'.

SQUEALER: Hip hip —

ALL THE ANIMALS: Hooray.

SQUEALER: Hip hip —

ALL THE ANIMALS: Hooray.

SQUEALER: Hip hip —

ALL THE ANIMALS: Hooray.

MINIMUS (*entering in great excitement*): Comrades, comrades, comrades!
I have a new poem. It is an ode to our father, Comrade Napoleon. It is entitled Comrade Napoleon.
Friend of the fatherless!
Fountain of happiness!
Lord of the swill bucket!
Oh, how my soul is on
Fire when I gaze at thy
Calm and commanding eye
Like the sun in the sky
Comrade Napoleon!
Comrade Napoleon!
Comrade Napole-ole-ole-ole-on!

NAPOLEON: I approve of this poem.

MINIMUS (*turning a somersault*): Yippee!

NAPOLEON: Such loyal sentiments are more than welcome in these treacherous times. I will reward you by appointing you my first Taster.

MINIMUS: What do I have to taste?

NAPOLEON: You will have the First Taste of every meal served to me. In case my enemies have poisoned it.
The lights change.

BOY: Early in the new year Animal Farm was proclaimed a Republic.

NAPOLEON: The president, who was elected unanimously, is me.

ALL THE ANIMALS: Comrade Napoleon!
Comrade Napoleon!
Comrade Napole-ole-ole-ole-on!
The PIGS *leave. Lights change.*

BOY: That night, the sound of loud singing came from the farmhouse . . .

PIGS (*drunk offstage*): Beasts of England, seize the prizes,
    Wheat and barley, oats and hay!

BOY: The pigs had for some time been using all the money to
    buy more and more whisky. At about half-past-nine,
    Napoleon, wearing Mr Jones' old bowler hat, galloped out
    of the house.

NAPOLEON: **On the dusty day when I was born**
    I was not very big.
    In fact, of a litter of seventeen,
    I was the smallest pig.
    It was more of a scramble than a birthday
    And I came out back to front.
    I was the last of the bunch
    When it came to lunch
    Yes, I was the litter's runt.

    But a runt has to fight
    For his share of the milk
    If he fancies staying alive.
    He'll kick with his feet
    And cling to the teat
    And the runt may yet survive.

    And if that young runt
    Grabs enough of the swill
    Then his bit will be worse than his grunt.
    He'll grow stately and stout
    With an eloquent snout
    But he knows he was the runt.

    (*His megalomania increases.*)
    And the runt seizes power
    For he knows all the tricks —
    Those he bites will never bite back.
    And the piglet who once
    Was the weakest of runts
    Shall be leader of the pack.
    Shall be the leader
    Shall be the leader
    Shall be the leader.

    I have created a new decoration: The Order of the Green
    Banner. I have conferred it on myself.
    Lights down.

BOY: And the very next morning, the attack came. The animals awoke to find that the men had surrounded the windmill in the night. It was clear they intended to blow it up.
Lights up.
The ANIMALS *look nervously at the distant windmill. It is surrounded by* MEN. *One is poised over an explosive plunger.*

NAPOLEN (*rallying them*): It's impossible! We have built the walls far too thick for that. Courage, comrades!
The plunger is driven home. A huge explosion. All the ANIMALS *fling themselves flat on the ground. The windmill is in ruins.*

BOY: Without waiting for any orders, the animals charged.

ALL THE ANIMALS: Charge!

BOY: They chased the men over the fields and off the farm.
The ANIMALS *stand among the ruins of the windmill.*

BOXER: Our windmill is gone. Even the foundations are destroyed.

CLOVER: It's as though it had never been.

ALL THE PIGS: Hooray!

BOXER (*amazed*): Why are you cheering?

SQUEALER: To celebrate our victory!

BOXER: What victory?

SQUEALER: What victory, comrade? Have we not driven the enemy off our soil, the sacred soil of Animal Farm?

BOXER: But they've destroyed our windmill. And we have worked on it for two years!

SQUEALER: What does it matter? We will build another windmill.

MINIMUS: And another windmill.

SQUEALER: We will build six windmills if we feel like it. You do not appreciate, comrade, the mighty thing that we have done. The enemy was in occupation of this very ground that we stand upon. And now — thanks to the leadership of Comrade Napoleon — we have won every inch of it back again.

BOXER: Then we have won back what we already had.

SQUEALER: Yes. That is our victory.
NAPOLEON *appears at the window.*

NAPOLEON: On this day of joy, you must hear the other good
news. There is now no more fear on Animal Farm. The
traitor Snowball has been eliminated. One of our comrades,
a Bull, who I will not name for reasons of security, is
enslaved on the farm where Snowball has been wallowing in
luxury. This hero broke into Snowball's sty and gored him
to death. Snowball is no more! You need be frightened no
longer.

MINIMUS: I shall write a poem about it!

NAPOLEON: Excellent!
The PIGS *exit.*

BOXER: For the first time, it occurs to me that I am getting old.

CLOVER: A horse's lungs do not last forever.

BOXER: They'll keep me going long enough to see the windmill
rebuilt.
Lights change. The ANIMALS *begin to rebuild the
windmill.*

ALL THE ANIMALS:
**There was a whacking great limestone boulder
But the animals worked as one.
Yes, through animal cooperation
Anything can be done!
Anything can be done!
Anything can be done!**
During the song, BOXER *collapses on the floor. The*
ANIMALS *gather round.*

CLOVER: Boxer! What is it?

BOXER: It's my lung. It doesn't matter. I think you'll be able
to finish the windmill now without me. There is a pretty
good store of stone.
Enter SQUEALER.

SQUEALER (*full of concern*): Comrade Napoleon has learned
with the deepest distress of this misfortune to one of the
most loyal workers on the farm. He is already making
arrangements to send Boxer to be treated in the village
hospital.

CLOVER: Why? I don't like animals leaving the farm.

BENJAMIN: And I don't like to think of a sick comrade in the
hands of human beings.

SQUEALER: The veterinary surgeon in the village can treat

Boxer's case more satisfactorily. It is the best thing for him.
BOXER *begins to struggle to his feet, helped by the other*
ANIMALS. *He reaches a kneeling position.*

BOXER: **I will be well, friends,**
And I'll retire, friends,
To the shadow of the chestnut tree
With time for thinking
And time for learning
The remainder of my ABC —
Um . . . D.

He struggles to his feet. Lights fade.

BOY: The next day, a van arrived to take Boxer away.
Lights up on a MAN *shutting the rear door of a*
horse-drawn van. He begins to lead the HORSE *out of the*
gate.

GLOVER: Goodbye, Boxer.

ALL THE ANIMALS (*quietly*): Goodbye, Boxer! Goodbye!
BENJAMIN *comes running in braying at the top of his*
voice.

BENJAMIN: Fools! Fools! Can't you see what is written on the
side of that van.
MURIEL *begins to spell out the words.*

MURIEL: Alfred Simmonds, Horse S L. . . . . . er, Horse S L. . .

BENJAMIN: Oh shut up! Let me read it. 'Alfred Simmonds,
Horse Slaughterer and Glue Boiler'. They are taking Boxer
to the knackers!

ALL THE ANIMALS: Boxer!
Cries of horror from the ANIMALS.

CLOVER: Boxer! Boxer! Get out! Get out quickly! They are
taking you to your death!

ALL THE ANIMALS: Boxer!
CLOVER *pleads with the* HORSE *pulling the van.*

CLOVER: Comrade, don't take your brother to his death.

ALL THE ANIMALS: Boxer!
BOXER's *face appears at the small window at the back of*
the van. He tries to kick his way out. The MAN *whips the*
HORSE *and the van moves down the road.*

BOY: In a few moments, the sound of drumming hoofs grew
fainter and died away. Three days later, Squealer made an
announcement.

Enter SQUEALER:

SQUEALER: It has come to my knowledge that a foolish and
wicked rumour has been circulating. Some of you noticed
that the van which took Boxer away was marked 'Horse
Slaughterer', and have actually come to the conclusion that
Boxer was being sent to the knackers. It is almost
unbelievable that any animal could be so stupid. Surely,
surely you know your beloved leader, Comrade Napoleon,
better than that? The explanation is really very simple. The
van had previously been the property of the knacker, and
had been bought by the veterinary surgeon who had not yet
painted the old name out. That was how the mistake arose.

CLOVER (*weeping*): I am very relieved to hear it.

MURIEL: So am I.

SQUEALER: Our beloved Comrade Boxer is dead. He died in the
village hospital in spite of receiving every attention a horse
could have.
NAPOLEON *appears drunk at the window of the
farmhouse.*

NAPOLEON: Comrades. It has not after all been possible to bring
back our lamented Comrade's remains. In a few days time,
we pigs intend to hold a memorial banquet in Boxer's
honour. Whisky will be drunk to his memory.

SQUEALER: I am happy to say that I was present during Boxer's
last hours. I was the most affecting sight I have ever seen.
'Forward Comrades', he whispered. 'Forward in the name
of the rebellion. Long live Animal Farm! Long live
Comrade Napoleon! Napoleon is always right'.

NAPOLEON: I believe those maxims are ones which every animal
would do well to adopt as his own.

CLOVER: Were those his last words?

SQUEALER: They were.

NAPOLEON: 'Napoleon is always right.'
All the ANIMALS *bow their heads in rememberance of*
BOXER. *They sing quietly. The lights begin to fade.*

ALL THE ANIMALS: **Napoleon is always right**
Always right, always right.
We will work harder.
We will work harder.
Lights change.

BOY: Years passed. Seasons came and went. The short animal
   lives fled by. Jones was dead — he had died in a home for
   drunks in another part of the country. The farm was more
   prosperous now. The windmill had been successfully rebuilt
   at last.
   The windmill is seen with its sails turning.
   But it was not after all used for generating electrical power.
   It was hired out for milling corn to neighbouring farmers
   and brought in a great deal of money. But the luxuries
   which Snowball had once taught the animals to dream of —
   the stall with electric light and hot and cold water, the
   three-day week — well, they were no longer talked about.
   NAPOLEON enters, fat and in full regalia.
   Napoleon was now a mature boar of twenty-four stone.
   One day the four sows all littered simultaneously,
   producing thirty-one young pigs between them. As
   Napoleon was now the only boar left on the farm, it was
   easy to guess at their parentage. Once again all rations were
   reduced. Only the pigs and dogs ate well.

SHEEP: Food! Where's our food! Give us food!

BENJAMIN: However much things change, they always remain
   the same.
   Lights up on the Sunday morning meeting. NAPOLEON
   addresses the ANIMALS.

NAPOLEON: **Armed to the teeth**
   We march along
   Bullets not barley
   We need
   Can't you hear the alarm?
   We'll save our farm
   Before we feed!

   As NAPOLEON *finishes his song, a tractor driven by a* PIG,
   with another PIG *standing behind him with a rifle, processes
   round the farmyard. As it goes off, the rifle is fired in a
   salute. An answering fusillade of rifle shots is heard off-stage.
   A large banner with a picture of* NAPOLEON's *head is
   unfurled.* NAPOLEON *and the* PIGS *go off.*
   There is a silence. The ANIMALS *are horrified.*

CLOVER: **This isn't what we wanted**
   This isn't what we meant
   When our great rebellion began.
   We hoped to make a farm where

> All animals were free
> Of hunger, whips and man.

MURIEL (*contradicting her*):
> You must be strong to grow Animalism
> Rake out the stones
> Rip out the weeds.
> We'll reap the harvest of Animalism
> Marching wherever
> Napoleon leads.

At least we work for ourselves. None of us goes upon two legs. None of us calls another creature Master. All Animals Are Equal.
Lights up on a line of PIGS *across the back of the stage. They are all dressed in incongruous bits of human clothing. Slowly they rise to their feet, and walk unsteadily round the stage on two feet.*

CLOVER: I think the world has been turned upside down.

BENJAMIN: I shall protest. For the first time in my life I shall protest. (*He confronts the* PIGS.) You pigs have gone far enough.

THE SHEEP: Four legs good
> Four legs good
> Two legs better!
> Two legs better!

The PIGS *join in the round and leave.*
The lights fade.
The stage is empty except for BENJAMIN *and* CLOVER. *They look at the wall at the end of the barn.*

CLOVER: My sight is failing. The wall looks different. Muriel, read what you see.

MURIEL: No, I won't. I will never read anything again.

CLOVER: Will you read it, Benjamin?

BENJAMIN: There's only one commandment now. And just this once I'll break my rule and read it to you. 'All animals are equal. But some animals are more equal than others.'
Lights change.

BOY: A week later, in the afternoon, a number of human visitors arrived at the farm.
A deputation of neighbouring FARMERS *enter. The* PIGS *welcome the humans effusively. There is much shaking of hands and trotters.*

BOY: The farmers were shown around and expressed great admiration for everything they saw. Especially the windmill.

ALL THE FARMERS (*in approval*): Ah!

PILKINGTON: Gentlemen, there was a time when the existence of a farm owned and operated by pigs was somehow felt to be abnormal. But what do I and my friends find here today? Not only the most up to date methods, but a discipline and an order which should be an example to all farmers everywhere. I believe indeed that the lower animals on Animal Farm do more work and receive less food than any animals in the country.

NAPOLEON: I too am happy that the period of misunderstanding is at an end. For a long time, there were rumours — circulated I have reason to believe, by some malignant enemy — that there was something subversive and even revolutionary in the outlook of myself and my colleagues. Nothing could be further from the truth!
Our sole wish, now and in the past, is to live at peace and in normal business relations with our neighbours.
Lights change.

BOY: That evening loud laughter and bursts of singing came from the farmhouse.
A long dinner table. The PIGS *and the* FARMERS *are at their after-dinner speeches.*

PILKINGTON (*on his feet*): And in conclusion, may I say that we have learnt a great deal here today.

BOY: What could be happening in there, now that for the first time, animals and human beings were meeting on terms of equality? All the other animals crept to the dining room window and peered and listened.
The other ANIMALS *gather round the window.*

PILKINGTON: Between pigs and human beings, there is not, and there need not be, any clash of interests whatever. Our struggles and our difficulties are the same. Is not the labour problem the same everywhere? If you have your lower animals, we have our lower classes! (*He laughs.*) And now gentlemen, and ladies, will you be upstanding? Gentlemen, I give you a toast: To the prosperity of Animal Farm.

PIGS *and* FARMERS: Animal Farm!
They all sit.

NAPOLEON (*rising*): I have only one criticism to make on
Mr Pilkington's excellent and neighbourly speech. He
referred throughout to 'Animal Farm'. Mr Pilkington
could of course not know — for I am announcing it now for
the first time — that the name Animal Farm has been
abolished. Henceforward, the farm is to be known as
Manor Farm. I believe that is its correct and original name.
Gentlemen, I give you the same toast as before, but in a
different form: To the prosperity of Manor Farm.

PIGS *and* FARMERS (*rising to toast*): Manor Farm!

PILKINGTON: More profit for fewer people!

SQUEALER: More power in fewer hands!

NAPOLEON: More control of beast and human!

FIRST FARMER: Use every inch of land!

PILKINGTON: I see the future
Shine on me
And pictures
Of the times to be —

Where chickens hatch
Ten thousand eggs
And never need
To stretch their legs

NAPOLEON: And sheep in crates
May spend their days
And grow us wool
But never graze.

FIRST FARMER: I see the future
Shine on me
And pictures
Of the times to be —

The silky mink
The fiery fox
Shall grow us fur
Inside a box

SQUEALER: And calves be born
Grow up, give birth,
And die but never
Walk on earth.

ALL: I see the future
Shine on me

And pictures
Of the times to be.
Where day and night
And heat and cold
And birth and death
Are all controlled
And profit rules
And all is calm
On England's grey
And modern farm.

And profit rules
And all is calm
On England's grey
And modern farm.

PILKINGTON: Science is a wonderful thing. In order to produce more meat and clothing, we men are developing a pig that can grow wool!

PIGS (*enraged*): What?
They strike the MEN.

NAPOLEON: We pigs are experimenting with a human being who will lay eggs.

HUMANS (*enraged*): What?
They strike the PIGS. *As each figure is hit, he moves slowly upstage, and once his back is to the audience, the mask is removed — whether* PIG *or* HUMAN. *The figure then turns round. For the first time, the naked human face is seen. Both* PIGS *and* MEN *are now unmasked.*

BOY: The creatures outside looked from pig to man, and from man to pig, and from pig to man again. But already it was impossible to say which was which.
The figures continue to stare out front.
The lights begin to fade.
The BOY *closes the book, replaces it in the bookcase, and walks slowly off the stage.*
The lights fade to darkness.

MUSIC

ADRIAN MITCHELL was born in London in 1932. On coming
down from Oxford he worked as a journalist before collaborating
with Peter Brook on *Marat/Sade* and *US* for the Royal
Shakespeare Company. He has published several novels and
collections of poetry and has given countless poetry readings in
Britain and abroad. His stage adaptations include *The Government
Inspector* (twice), *The Good Woman*, *The Mayor of Zalamea*
and *Peer Gynt*. His stage shows have been performed by, among
others, the National Theatre (*Tyger*), 7:84 (*Man Friday*), The
Liverpool Everyman (*Mind Your Head*) and The Nottingham
Playhouse (*White Suit Blues*). He wrote *Uppendown Mooney*
and *King Real* for Welfare State International and has also
contributed songs to their *Raising the Titanic*. He has written
librettos for three operas and a version of *The Magic Flute* for
Peter Hall at Covent Garden. He was screenwriter on the films
of *Marat/Sade* and *Man Friday*, while his television plays include
Cavalcade, Can't Laugh, Man Friday, Total Disaster and two plays
in the BBC's *Churchill's People*.

RICHARD PEASLEE, a native of New York, has written
extensively for the theatre in England and America. He composed
the music for the Peter Brook/Royal Shakespeare Company
productions of *Marat/Sade, A Midsummer Night's Dream, US,
Antony and Cleopatra* and *Oedipus*. His music for Martha Clark's
Garden of Earthly Delights won him an Obie. Other scores for
Broadway and Off-Broadway productions include *Indians,
Boccaccio, Marigolds, Frankenstein, Cinders* and *The Children's
Crusade*. He has also written music for Joe Papp's Shakespeare-
in-the-Park and leading regional theatres such as the Guthrie,
Arena, ART and the Yale Rep. He has composed extensively for
William Russo's London Jazz Orchestra and Joseph Chaikin's
Open Theatre productions as well as working with Twyla Tharp,
the Joffrey Ballet and the Kathryn Posin Dance Company. He has
had concert works performed by a variety of artists ranging from
Gerry Mulligan to the Philadelphia Orchestra. Film and Television
credits include *Tell Me Lies, Where Time is a River* and the
Time/Life series *Wild Wild World of Animals*.

MAN'S HYMN TO MAN

BEASTS OF ENGLAND

(♩ = 112)

OLD MAJOR:

BEASTS OF ENG - LAND BEASTS OF IRE - LAND

BEASTS OF LAND AND SEA AND SKIES ___ HEAR THE HOOF - BEATS

OF TO - MOR - ROW SEE THE GOLD - EN FUT - URE RISE ___

CHORUS/OLD MAJOR (QUIET BUT INTENSE)

NOW THE DAY OF BEASTS IS COM - ING ___ TY - RANT

BEASTS OF ENGLAND (continued)

MAN SHALL LOSE HIS THRONE___ AND THE SHIN - ING FIELDS OF

ENG - LAND___ SHALL BE TROD BY BEASTS A - LONE.___

PULL THE RINGS FROM OUT YOUR NOS - ES TEAR THE SAD - DLE

FROM YOUR BACK__ BIT AND SPUR SHALL RUST FOR - EV - ER

OLD MAJOR

(♩ = 88)

OLD MAJOR:

HOW DOES THE LIFE OF AN AN-I-MAL PASS? _ IN END-LESS

DRUDG-ER-Y _ WHAT'S THE FIRST LES-SON AN AN-I-MAL LEARNS? _ TO EN-DURE ITS

SLAV-ER-Y _ HOW DOES THE LIFE OF AN AN-I-MAL END? _ IN CRU-EL

OLD MAJOR (continued)

ANIMALISM

NO MAN, NO MASTER

NO MAN, NO MASTER (continued)

SUGAR CANDY MOUNTAIN

SUGAR CANDY MOUNTAIN (continued)

SUGAR CANDY MOUNTAIN (continued)

SUGAR CANDY MOUNTAIN (continued)

NO SWEET BYE- AND - BYE _____ THERE'S NO SUCH PLACE AS

SUG - AR CAN-DY MOUN-TAIN. SUG-AR CAN-DY MOUN-TAIN IS A LIE, LIE, LIE, LIE_

SUG - AR CAN-DY MOUN-TAIN IS A LIE _____ THERE'S NO SUCH PLACE AS SUG-AR CAN-DY

SUGAR CANDY MOUNTAIN (continued)

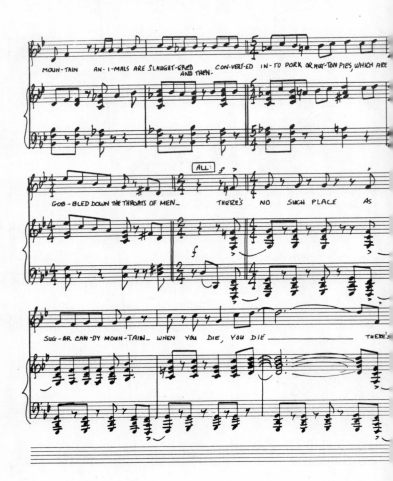

MOUN-TAIN AN-I-MALS ARE SLAUGHT-ERED AND THEN- CON-VERT-ED IN-TO PORK OR MUT-TON PIES, WHICH ARE

GOB-BLED DOWN THE THROATS OF MEN_ THERE'S NO SUCH PLACE AS

SUG-AR CAN-DY MOUN-TAIN_ WHEN YOU DIE, YOU DIE_____ THERE'S

ANIMAL FARM

THE SEVEN COMMANDMENTS

THE SEVEN COMMANDMENTS (continued)

THE GREEN FLAG

OUR LAND WAS ONCE A FOR-EST__ ALL GREEN FROM SHORE TO SHORE__ TILL HU-MANS TORE THE GREEN-WOOD DOWN WITH AXE AND FIRE AND SAW___ BUT

FOUR LEGS GOOD

LIVELY ($\quad$ = 128-132)

SUNG BY ALL AS A
THREE PART ROUND

FOUR LEGS GOOD — FOUR LEGS GOOD — TWO LEGS BAD — TWO LEGS BAD —

FOUR LEGS GOOD — TWO LEGS BAD — FOUR LEGS GOOD AND

TWO LEGS BAD ———

* = ENTRANCES

SNOWBALL ON THE FUTURE

TWENTY-SEVEN RIBBONS (continued)

TWENTY-SEVEN RIBBONS

A VOTE FOR SNOWBALL

LONG LIVE ANIMAL FARM

THE BOULDER SONG

THE BOULDER SONG (continued)

SHE CAME AT THE RUN __ WE TRIED TO MOVE THAT LIME-STONE

BOUL-DER __ (UHH!) COULD-N'T BE DONE __ WE AP-PEALED TO THE SHEEP COM-MIT-TEE __

CALLED UP THE GOATS BRI-GADE __ AND THE CHICK-ENS AND THE GEESE TO SHIFT THAT ROCK __ (UNH!)

BUT IT JUST STAYED __ IT JUST STAYED WHERE IT WAS THAT GREAT

THE BOULDER SONG (continued)

THE BOULDER SONG (continued)

HEART AND SOUL _ AND THAT WHACK-ING GREAT BOUL -DER START-ED TO ROLL, AND

ROLL, AND ROLL, AND ROLL _____ (INTO CHEERS

(CHEERS) _____

(CUT OFF BY FX CRASH)

(CUT OFF BY FX CRASH)

V.S.

THE BOULDER SONG (continued)

WORK SONG

THE HEN'S REVOLT

THE HEN'S REVOLT (continued)

THE HEN'S REVOLT (continued)

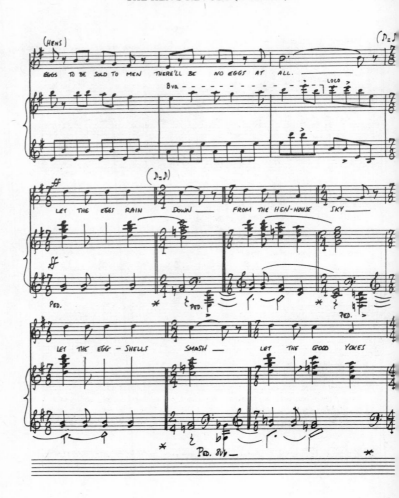

EGGS TO BE SOLD TO MEN THERE'LL BE NO EGGS AT ALL.

LET THE EGGS RAIN DOWN FROM THE HEN-HOUSE SKY

LET THE EGG-SHELLS SMASH LET THE GOOD YOKES

THE HEN'S REVOLT (continued)

THE HEN'S REVOLT (continued)

THE HEN'S REVOLT (continued)

A NOTHING SONG

A NOTHING SONG (continued)

A NOTHING SONG (continued)

A NOTHING SONG (continued)

THE GREEN FLAG: MINIMUS' VERSION

SQUEALER EXPLAINS

COMRADE NAPOLEON

COMRADE NAPOLEON (continued)

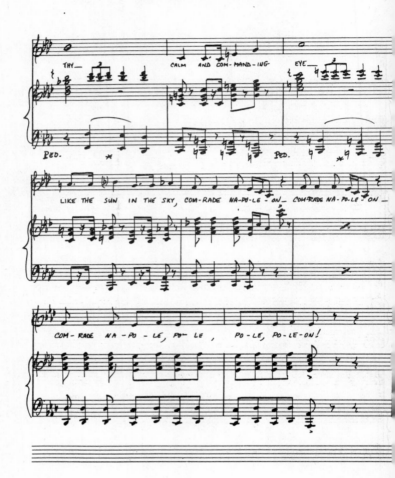

RUNT OF THE LITTER

RUNT MAY YET SUR - VIVE ____ AND IF THAT YOUNG RUNT GRABS E -

- NOUGH OF THE SWILL THEN HIS BITE WILL BE WORSE THAN HIS GRUNT ____ HE'LL GROW

STATE-LY AND STOUT WITH AN EL-O-QUENT SNOUT BUT HE KNOWS HE WAS THE ____

ANYTHING CAN BE DONE

DOGGEDLY (♩ = 108)

ANIMALS

THERE WAS A WHACK-ING GREAT LIME-STONE BOUL-DER ___ BUT AN-I-MALS WORKED AS ONE ___ BE-CAUSE THROUGH AN-I-MAL CO-OP-ER-A-TION ___ AN-Y-THING CAN BE DONE ___ AN-Y-THING CAN BE DONE ___ AN-Y-THING CAN BE DONE. ___

BOXER'S SONG

SIMPLY (♩ = 66)

I WILL BE WELL, FRIENDS AND I'LL RE-TIRE, FRIENDS TO THE SHAD-OW OF THE CHEST-NUT TREE WITH TIME FOR THINK-ING AND TIME FOR LEARN-ING THE RE-MAIN-DER OF MY A - B - C THE RE-MAIN-DER OF MY A - B - C. (SPOKEN:) "UHM....D"

DETERMINED CHORUS

NAPOLEON RALLIES THE RANKS

SCHMALTZY (♩ = 66)

NAPOLEON

ARMED TO THE TEETH WE MARCH A - LONG ___

BUL-LETS ___ NOT BAR-LEY WE NEED ___ CAN'T YOU HEAR THE A - LARM ___ WE'LL

SAVE OUR FARM ___ WE MUST FIGHT BE - FORE WE

NAPOLEON RALLIES THE RANKS (continued)

SOMETHING BURNING

(♩ = 96)

CLOVER   mf

I CAN SEE THE WHOLE OF THE

FARM FROM HERE _ AND THE FARM NEV-ER LOOKED SO DE-SIR-A-BLE _ THE

HAY-FIELD, THE SPIN-NEY AND THE DRINK-ING POOL _ THE YOUNG WHEAT GREEN _ AND

LEAP-ING _ GRASS AND BURST-ING HEDG-ES GUILD-ED BY THE SUN _ OF A

POSSIBLE CUT

SOMETHING BURNING (continued)

CLEAR, CALM SPRING-TIME EVE-NING___ I CAN SEE THE WHOLE OF THE FARM FROM HERE___ AND I CAN SMELL SOME - THING BURN-ING. _____

THIS ISN'T WHAT WE WANTED

THIS IS-N'T WHAT WE WANT-ED THIS IS-N'T WHAT WE

THIS ISN'T WHAT WE WANTED (continued)

THIS ISN'T WHAT WE WANTED (continued)

THIS ISN'T WHAT WE WANTED (continued)

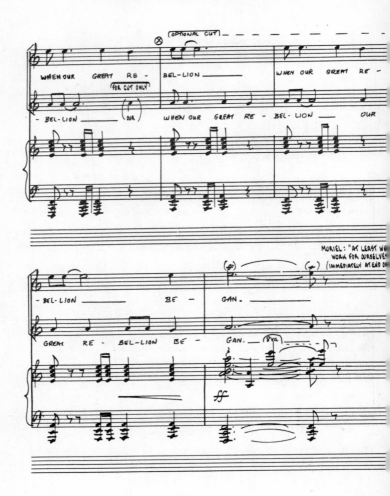

TWO LEGS BETTER

I SEE THE FUTURE

RAUCOUS (♩ = 116)

PILKINGTON

I SEE THE FU-TURE SHINE

ME ___ AND PIC-TURES OF THE ___ TIMES TO BE ___ WHE

NAPOLEON

CHICK-ENS HATCH TEN THOUS-AND EGGS AND NEV-ER NEED ___ TO STRETCH THEIR LEGS

I SEE THE FUTURE (continued)

SHEEP IN CRATES MAY SPEND THEIR DAYS—
AND GROW US WOOL BUT NEV-ER GRAZE—

(CHEERING)

(CHEERING)

2ND FARMER

I SEE THE FU-TURE SHINE ON ME— AND

PIC-TURES OF THE— TIMES TO BE— THE SILK-Y MINK, THE FIE-RY FOX SHALL

SQUEALER

GROW US FUR IN-SIDE A BOX — AND CALVES BE BORN— AND GROW UP GIVE BIRTH —

I SEE THE FUTURE (continued)

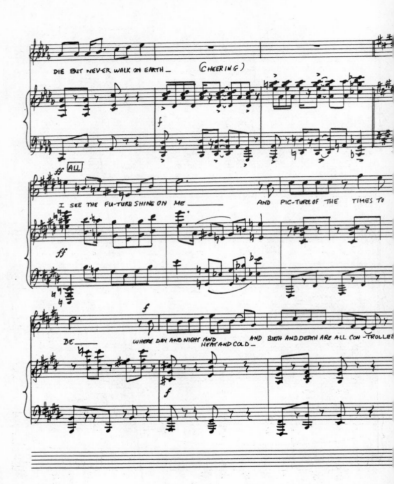

DIE BUT NEV-ER WALK ON EARTH _ (CHEERING)

I SEE THE FU-TURE SHINE ON ME _____ AND PIC-TURE OF THE TIMES TO

BE _ WHERE DAY AND NIGHT AND HEAT AND COLD _ AND BIRTH AND DEATH ARE ALL CON -TROLLED

I SEE THE FUTURE (continued)